The Legend of Vartanis I

The Legend of Vartanis

by Emmanuel Jean-Pierre

Illustrated by Jessica Bryant

To Rosie Sanchez, who loved The Book of Elyon so much, it inspired me to write a story for little girls.

Acknowledgements

Lou and Rosie Sanchez, who read the first drafts and gave me suggestions

My wife Yolanda Jean-Pierre for letting me read it to her

The Valley Cottage writers group and the Nyack Library writers group for their invaluable critiques

Jessica Bryant for lending her wondrous artistic abilities for the illustrations

Kindle Direct Publishing for making the printing possible

Chapter one

There once was a kingdom named Vartanis where everyone lived in perfect harmony. Men and women, boys and girls, lions and lambs, and dragons and dolphins, all lived and played together.

It was always spring and never winter in Vartanis. There were forests with leaves of every color under the Sun: red, orange, yellow, and even joy. What was that? Joy isn't a color? Well, it is in Vartanis. So are peace, laughter, and love and every forest was painted with them.

However, what made this kingdom so special wasn't that the animals got along. It wasn't that dragons helped humans cook their meals. It wasn't that emotions had colors. It wasn't even that lions gave babies piggy back rides. No, what made this kingdom extra special was that everyone had a very unique power.

See, in Vartanis all the men and boys had the ability to control water. They used this power to make wonderful things like floating waterfalls and river roller coasters they would ride with the dolphins and sea lions.

All the women and girls on the other hand had the ability to make fire. They used this power to make wonderful things as well like fiery tornadoes and wings made of flames so they could play with the dragons.

Now you might be wondering: how in the world did fire and water get along so well? That, my friend, was the wonder of the kingdom. The boys and girls would put their powers together to make fantastic things like hot tubs in the middle of forests, water slides on the sides of volcanoes, and play fire dodgeball and water tag.

Everyone lived and worked together in harmony: men and women, children and adults, fire and water. Everything was perfect.

However, there was one creature in Vartanis who didn't like this harmony: the evil Sea Serpent. It hated it all so much that one day it changed everything forever.

The Sea Serpent convinced a group of boys that girls were weak and unnecessary because, of course, fire could never beat water. He convinced them that girls should never be allowed to do anything that boys could do and that they should be servants instead. So with time, this group grew to hate girls and made plans to make all girls their servants. They called themselves the Crystal Lords.

One day, when they had rallied all the boys in Vartanis on their side, the Crystal Lords waged war on all the women and girls, drowning everyone who tried to stop them. The women and girls fought bravely, but fire could never beat water. Sadly, in one dramatic sweep, the Crystal Lords flooded all of Vartanis then froze the kingdom. In the aftermath of the war, the Crystal Lords and other boys like them became rulers and all the women and girls became their servants. Vartanis went from being a kingdom to being an empire and a young Crystal Lord named Andrew became the emperor. He renamed Vartanis Andromeno.

While Vartanis was filled with life and balance between men and women, children and adults, and dragons and dolphins, Andromeno was an empire of division. Gone were the endless springs, volcano water slides, and river roller coasters. Instead, the Crystal Lords froze the entire empire until everything was made entirely of ice. It was stunningly beautiful, but also unbearably cold, making it impossible for most of the animals to survive. So all the dragons, dolphins, lions, and lambs migrated far, far away from the cold empire of Andromeno never to be seen again.

But there was a prophecy that one day a Chosen One would be born that would bring down the empire and restore the kingdom. What is the difference between a kingdom and an empire, you ask? You'll have to keep reading to find out...

Chapter two

Several hundred years later, the empire of Andromeno was quite a different place from the Vartanis I just described to you. First of all, as I said before, everything was made of ice: ice hammers, ice shovels, ice houses, and ice mansions. As cold as it was, it was all undeniably beautiful. Whenever the sunlight shone through a window or a building, there would be blinding explosions of colors, like rainbows bouncing off the ice.

In the very center of this empire was a city made of crystals called the Imperial City, with a palace made of crystal called the Imperial Palace, which was at the foot of a giant mountain made of crystal called—you guessed it—the Crystal Mountain.

Outside the Imperial City, however, were poor villages where people lived in igloos. In the poorest village of them all, in the smallest igloo of them all, was a particular family that was very ordinary and very much unimportant to everyone around them. But they are very important to us in this story. At this moment we find them at the Imperial City in the middle of the most important day of the year in Andromeno: the Rain Ceremony.

Christina, Caroline, Cindy, and Dominic followed their mother through a raging crowd of roaring boys and men who shoved them, pulled at them, and sprayed streams of water at them as they walked past.

"Fire is danger, water is justice!" the boys chanted. "Every girl's a stranger! Leave till it's just us!"

"Yeah!" Dominic cheered, throwing his fist in the air. He shoved Caroline then cheered in her face, "Fire is danger, water is justice!"

Caroline shoved him back and two flames flashed to life in her hands. "Touch me again and I'll show you danger!"

"Knock it off!" Mother ordered them, stepping in between them. "We're almost at the altar." She continued walking, struggling to balance the bowl of crabs in one arm while holding little Cindy's hand. Dom followed close behind her, sticking his tongue out at Caroline as he went.

Caroline stuck her tongue back then scoffed to Christina.

"He's such a loser," she muttered.

Christina nodded. "I can't believe he's our brother."

The chants went on as they continued through the city and boys scowled at the girls as they walked past, booing them, spitting at them, and making obscene gestures that are too shameful for me to describe. Christina made her hands into fists as she walked. She always got so angry seeing how mean boys were to girls.

The family finally made it to the altars and paused behind the line at one of them. Christina and Caroline took in the view as they waited, staring at the ice statues of Emperor Andrew lined up on either side of the Palace entrance. They were all more than twenty feet tall and had him with his hands on his hips and staring up into the sky with a grave look on his face. Even in the moonlight, the statues sparkled like diamonds.

"Mommy, the statue is pretty!" little Cindy exclaimed, pointing.

Caroline spit in the snow. "Pretty *stupid.*"

"It is, sweetie," Mother replied. "Caroline, watch your mouth."

"Yeah," Dominic added. "You want me to freeze it for her, Mother?"

Caroline stepped up to him immediately. "I'd like to see you try, you little snowflake!"

"C'mon at me, sis!" Dominic taunted, already raising the snow around him into miniature tornadoes.

Caroline held two flames in her hands, ready to blast her brother.

"Caroline!' Mother cried. "Stand down!"

Caroline stared at Dom, who smirked back at her, allowing the snow tornadoes to spiral around him. She huffed angrily, then shut her hands and her flames went out.

"You're lucky it's an eclipse," she threatened. "On any other day, you'd be toast."

Mother reached the front of the line and poured the crabs onto the pile of other crabs on top of the altar then turned left and joined a crowd of girls and women standing at the opposite end of the altars. Dom turned right and joined the crowd of boys and men standing on the opposite end.

"At least he's gone now," Caroline said.

"But we're still here," Christine replied. "Why do we have to be here? This isn't right."

As they watched, a group of servant girls in blue hooded parkas stepped up to the altars. The girls held their hands out and set the altars ablaze one by one, lighting up the front of the Palace like giant torches in the night.

Christina felt the hair on the back of her neck rise. Despite the bitter cold of the night air, she could still feel the chills of fear run up her spine. She did not want to witness what was about to happen again. Nor did she want to feel what would come after.

"Mother, why doesn't someone stop this?" she asked.

"It's the way of the empire," Mother replied. "We can't stop it."

"Then can we go home? I don't want to go through this again."

Before Mother could reply, the crowd went silent as the Palace doors swung open. The Ceremony was about to begin.

Chapter three

Two adult men in royal blue robes stepped out of the Palace and approached the waiting crowd. Behind them trailed a young boy in a matching royal blue robe, a blue sash draped over one of his shoulders, and a golden crown on his head. He was no more than fourteen years old and this was obvious by his pale, pimple-ridden skin, and how he was puffing his chest out and trying so desperately to mimic the way the men walked before him. This was Emperor Andrew. Not the same emperor you heard of at the beginning of this story, of course. This was, in actuality, Emperor Andrew the 47th, but he was simply referred to as Emperor Andrew for simplicity.

He and the two men came to a stop in front of the crowd and the boys and men cheered so loudly that their voices shook the ground. Caroline and Christina covered their ears and were grateful when Emperor Andrew raised his hand and everyone went silent.

"Thank you for coming to my first Rain Ceremony as your new Emperor," he said. "And thank you for all the crabs. They look very...dead."

There was a moment of confused silence.

"Excuse the Emperor," one of the men next to him interrupted. "He's still new to this."

"Go, Marcus!" a Crystal Lord in the crowd cheered.

Marcus grinned then looked back and forth from the men's side to the women's side.

"The moment you've all been waiting for has arrived," he began. "The Challenge."

The boys and men roared again and threw blasts of water and ice into the air. The girls and women around Caroline and Christina lowered their heads in silence.

"Boys get their power from the moon," Marcus continued. "Girls get their powers from the Sun. So the Rain Ceremony takes place every year on a full moon to remind us all that boys are better than girls. Because water always beats fire."

Caroline scoffed to Christina. "Then they should make it in the middle of the day so we can toast these suckers."

"But every year," Marcus continued. "Because boys and men are so merciful, the empire offers the girls a chance to challenge the boys. The bravest girl will face the bravest Crystal Lord. If the girl wins, it will prove that girls are stronger and for the next year they will rule instead."

"Boooo!" the boys cried.

"But..." Marcus interrupted them. "If the Crystal Lord wins, the girl will be exiled to the tundra where she'll be sentenced to freeze to death."

The boys cheered and sent more water and ice shooting into the sky.

Marcus stretched his arm to the side and a Crystal Lord stepped forward from the crowd of boys and stood next to him. He was as tall as Marcus, but his arms were much larger, with biceps the size of melons and a chest swelling underneath his blue tunic.

Marcus slapped his hand on the Crystal Lord's back then faced the girls' side.

"Do we have a challenger?" he asked.

Everyone waited in tense silence. It was so quiet Christina thought she could Caroline's heart beating next to her. Then, to her surprise, Caroline pushed Christina aside and took a step forward. But before she could get very far, Mother snatched her arm and yanked her back into the crowd.

"Get back here!" she scolded her.

"Let me go!" Caroline replied, trying to wrestle her arm free.

"I am not losing my oldest daughter to the tundra," Mother replied. "You stay put."

Caroline folded her arms across her chest and pouted as she waited.

Seconds wore into minutes with no one daring to move an inch. The Crystal Lord yawned with boredom and Emperor Andrew fidgeted nervously where he stood. Then Marcus raised his hand to announce that no challenge would be taken, but suddenly a teenage girl ran into the open.

"I challenge him!" she shouted.

The girls and women gasped. Some cheered. Others murmured. All of them stepped back to make room.

Marcus grinned a sinister grin then glanced at the Crystal Lord.

The Crystal Lord sauntered over to the girl and they stood between the two crowds.

"Challenge accepted," he said.

With that, the fight began. The girl sprang into action with a flurry of fireballs, but the Crystal Lord evaded them easily. She threw sheets of flames at him, but he put them out with streams of water before they could touch him. They went on for a mere minute with the girl fighting with all her might and the Crystal Lord dancing around her, teasing her as he went. The boys cheered, but the girls held their breath.

Then, after a little more than a minute into the fight, the Crystal Lord tripped the girl and she fell flat on her face. She recovered quickly and turned with her palms out, ready to blast fire into him. But the Crystal Lord aimed his hand at her and sent a burst of water into her chest, soaking her entire upper body. She dropped her hands, lowered her head, and began to sob. For now, dripping from head to toe in freezing water, her powers had been put out. She would no longer be able to make fire until she was dry again.

The boys cheered and the Crystal Lord turned to them, flexing his biceps.

Emperor Andrew clapped his hands then twirled his fingers in a circle. On cue, a giant falcon swooped down from above and grabbed the girl's shoulders in its talons.

"No!" she shrieked. "Please, give me another chance!"

But the bird paid her no mind and without any delay, it flapped its massive wings, took off into the air, and flew away with the girl screaming for her life.

Once she was gone, the boys looked to the sky in unison. The moon, which was normally as white as snow, had turned a bright, glowing red, as if it had been dipped in blood. The eclipse had begun.

The boys raised their hands and Christina watched as their eyes began to glow with blue light. She saw Dom staring straight at her and grinning maniacally. Her stomach turned in anticipation of what would happen next.

Clouds rolled across the sky, thick, gray, and as angry as the looks on the boys' faces. There was a crack of thunder and rain began to pour. But the rain only fell on the girls and women, leaving the boys and men dry on the other side. It rained for several minutes until the girls and women were so soaked that their coats were sticking to their skin.

Emperor Andrew lowered his hands and everyone else followed suit as they released the loudest roar of the night.

"Fire is danger! Water is justice! Every girl's a stranger. Leave till it's just us!"

Caroline and Christina rubbed their arms furiously, trembling from the ice cold water.

Caroline turned to her sister, huffing like an angry bull, and made her a promise.

"One day," she told her. "We're gonna end this. Once and for all."

Chapter four

Several months later, Caroline, Christina, and Cindy were playing outside of their igloo. I realize now that I haven't had a chance to properly introduce their family to you, so I will do so now. The father worked very hard in the Palace as one of the cleaners who washed the Emperor's clothes. The mother stayed home with her son and three daughters and cooked food all day and fed the family all night. Caroline was the oldest daughter at ten years old. She was quite a fireball, this one, as you've already seen, and not just because she could make fire like all girls. She was very strong-willed, outspoken, and never let anyone push her around, especially not her older brother Dominic. The youngest daughter was Cindy, who was six years old, and was quite the opposite of her older sister. While Caroline never let anyone tell her what to do, Cindy did anything anyone told her because she never wanted to make anyone unhappy.

Then there was the middle daughter, Christina, who was eight years old and didn't always know what to do. She didn't want to let people push her around like Cindy did, but she was too afraid to speak up like Caroline. So she would go back and forth from being brave then afraid, speaking and being silent until one day something happened that changed all of that. But we'll get to that soon.

On this particular day we find the three sisters playing behind their igloo. It was noon so the Sun was as high as it could be and the day was as warm as it could be(which was still quite cold, but not freezing like it usually was).

Despite the relative warm weather, the girls were still wearing their hooded parkas and boots they wore every day.

"You're it!" Caroline shouted as she tossed a fireball at Christina.

Christina laughed and ran after her, throwing fireballs back at her. But Caroline was much too swift and dodged all of them. So Christina turned and chased Cindy instead. She hit her baby sister with a small flame and she dropped on her bottom onto the snow.

"You're it!" Christina laughed.

But Cindy didn't think it was funny and immediately crossed her arms and started to cry.

"It's not fair!" she shouted.

Caroline walked over and stared down at her. "Stop being a baby, Cindy. It's just a game."

"You always tag me!" Cindy whined.

"Nobody likes a whiner," Caroline told her. "Wipe your tears."

Cindy sniffled a few more times then wiped her face because she didn't want anyone not to like her.

"Tag me back," Christina offered as she held her hand out.

"No, Chris!" Caroline shouted, slapping Christina's hand away. "She has to toughen up."

"But she's so little. I shouldn't have tagged her. Maybe we can just run a little slower."

"You're treating her like she's a little girl!"

"She *is* a little girl."

"Girls, settle down," Mother scolded them as she approached them. "It's noon. Line up."

Caroline groaned as her and her sisters lined up on either side of their mother for their daily ritual.

"Can we at least say the prophecy this time?" she asked.

Mother sighed deeply, but relented. "Yes, Caroline, you can say the prophecy."

At this, Caroline's demeanor brightened and her and her sisters raised their hands to the Sun. Then, all at once, the girls recited,

"Today the empire's run
By boys who kill all the fun
But the frozen will fall
When the Chosen One calls
And then the kingdom will come."

They kept their hands in the air, as if they were attempting to catch the Sun in case it fell out of the sky.

"Why do we do this again?" Cindy asked.

"Because our powers come from the Sun," Mother explained. "And the Sun is brightest at noon. So we reach up to receive power so that we can have more fire to cook for the boys and men."

Caroline rolled her eyes.

"Ooooh!" Cindy cried. "I feel it! I feel it!"

Christina wriggled her fingers. She could feel a slight warmth on her palms, but wasn't sure if that was an increase in her powers or simply the warmth of the sunlight.

"I don't feel anything," Caroline muttered.

"Maybe there's something wrong with your hands," Cindy said.

"Maybe there's something wrong with the Sun," Caroline countered.

"Come now," Mother said. "It's time to make lunch." She walked back towards the igloo and Cindy pranced happily behind her.

Caroline lowered her hands then looked at Christina. "You didn't feel anything, either, did you?"

Christina sighed. "No. But maybe I just wasn't doing it right. Maybe if I just practiced more I'd get it."

"You'll never get it," a voice said behind them. When they turned they saw Dominic walking towards them. He was dressed in the traditional blue tunic that all boys wore in the empire and had a blue bandana on his head that let everyone know he was training to become a Crystal Lord. He, as you can tell, wasn't wearing a parka because boys didn't get cold. As if to further prove this, he was carrying a canteen of ice cold water and took a swig as he stopped in front of his sisters.

"What do you want?" Christina asked.

"You heard Mother," he replied. "It's time for lunch. So get inside. And make it."

"You can't tell us what to do, Dom," Caroline spat. "We'll go in *if* and *when* we want to."

"Why do we go through this every day, Carol?"

"Because you're a jerk every day!" Caroline shouted. "And stop calling me that!"

"You should really be nicer to me," Dom snickered. "Or I'll make it rain on you."

"In your dreams!" Caroline replied. "The next full moon isn't for weeks, but the Sun is out now so I can roast you right here."

This was very true. Even though boys could control water, they could only make it rain during a full moon or an eclipse and even then only for a short while. This was why the rain during the last Rain Ceremony had been so powerful--it had occurred during a full moon *and* an eclipse.

"Maybe we should just go in," Christina offered. She didn't like when Caroline and Dom fought because it never ended well.

"Yeah," Dom agreed. "I'm hungry. Go make a sandwich. Then sing me a song, Carol."

"Make your own sandwich," Caroline spat. "You're not the boss of us."

"Actually, I am," Dom replied. "This is Andromeno. Boys rule. And girls...make sandwiches."

"That doesn't rhyme," Christina said.

"You know what else doesn't rhyme?" Dom asked her. "Your face!"

"That's it!" Caroline screamed. Like I said before, she was quite a fireball and not just because she could make fire—but because of her temper. Her hands suddenly flashed red and there were blazes of fire on her fists. She pulled one fist back to toss the biggest fireball of the day at Dom's head, but Dom reacted quicker than she had expected. Before she could launch the fireball, he held his hand out and shot a stream of water at her that drenched her body from her head to her toes.

Caroline's fire instantly went out with a sizzle and she stood there, very wet and still very angry. But now she had no fire to fight back with because as you've probably already guessed, it's very difficult to start a fire with wet hands. So all she could do was stand there and squeal angrily with gallons of water dripping off of her.

Dom pointed and laughed at her. "When will you learn, Carol? Boys are better than girls. Because water always beats fire." He took another swig of water and a green glimmer flashed across his eyes. Then he flicked his finger and splashed a drop of water onto

Caroline's face. "Now hurry up—I'm hungry." Then he turned and walked away.

Christina waited until Dom was out of earshot then touched her sister's arm and asked, "Are you okay?"

Caroline yanked her arm away. "Why didn't you do something?! If you had helped me, we could've fought back!"

"I thought..." Christina started. "I thought that...maybe if...I just don't think that..." She tried to say something that made sense, but the truth was she didn't know why she hadn't helped. Some days she was brave and some days she wasn't. Today had been one of the days that she wasn't.

Caroline shook her hands to try to dry them then started wringing the water out of her dreadlocks. She was huffing angrily, but Christina was almost sure that she saw tears in her eyes. But Caroline shook her head quickly and wiped away any emotion off of her face. Then she took a breath, faced Christina, and told her, "When it comes to boys, you either fight back or you let them bully you. Make a choice."

Then she turned and walked towards the igloo.

That day Caroline taught Christina that there were only two ways of dealing with boys: beating them or letting them beat her. But Christina wondered if there was a third choice.

Chapter five

While Dom was back in the igloo daydreaming about the sandwich his sisters were supposed to be making for him, Caroline and Christina were cooking up something much different for him outside.

Caroline led her sister to a group of evergreen trees not too far from the village, carrying a rope coiled around her shoulder. The trees were powdered white with snow and the ground was littered with gray rock and ice. Caroline stopped somewhere in the center of this small grove of trees at a patch of cracked gray rock.

"Here's your chance to get Dom back," she said as she turned to her sister. "Are you with me this time or are you gonna chicken out again?"

Christina shook her head. "I'm with you. I mean..." She stopped and nodded instead. "I'm with you."

"Good," Caroline grinned. She looked down at the gray rock. "Do you know what this is?"

Christina looked down at the rock and shrugged. She thought it looked like the back of a giant turtle, but she knew that it wasn't.

"Never mind," Caroline said. "Look." She knelt close to the ground and held her hands over the rock like she was touching the top of an invisible table. "Can you feel that?"

Christina imitated her sister's motions and tried to feel what she was feeling, but felt nothing. "No. What am I supposed to feel?"

Caroline sighed. "Come on. Keep trying."

Christina scrunched her face and tried to force herself to feel something. Then, just when it started to feel like she was constipated, she felt it. Heat. Her hands were sensing intense heat somewhere nearby.

"There's heat!" she shouted.

"Yeah," Caroline grinned mischievously. "There's heat underground."

"Really? But why? How?"

"I don't know. But you know what else is under there?"

"What?" Christina asked, eyes wide with anticipation.

"Water. And when water and heat get together, you know what happens?" She crashed her fingers together and made an imaginary explosion with her hands. "A geyser."

Christina gasped. "Whoaaaaa."

"If we make the heat hotter, we can make the geyser erupt. Come on. Follow my lead."

Caroline held her hands over the ground again and began a peculiar motion Christina had never seen her do before. She was pulling her hands back and forth as if she were folding and unfolding an invisible blanket.

"Come on," Caroline told her. "You can do it."

So Christina followed her sister's motions as carefully as she could. But Caroline's movements were so fluid and so smooth and Christina's appeared so clumsy. Worst of all, Christina couldn't feel the heat getting any hotter on her side. So finally, after only a few seconds of trying, she dropped her hands.

"I can't do it," she said.

"Come on, Chris," Caroline scolded her. "Stop trying to be perfect and just do it."

Christina sucked in her breath, resisting the urge to turn around and walk away. The only thing she hated more than not doing something well was disappointing her sister. She wanted so much to be like her, to be consistently strong like her, consistently brave like her, and consistently confident like her. She even wanted her hair too be in thick locks like her and her skin to be as bronze as hers. But Christina was only sporadically brave, her hair was finer, and her skin was much darker. But she didn't like spoiling opportunities to prove herself to her sister.

So she lifted her hands again and rolled them back and forth. But this time she didn't try to do it as perfectly as Caroline was and simply focused on doing it. Soon, sure enough, she felt the heat rising underground.

"I'm doing it!" she shouted.

"Told you!" Caroline replied.

They rolled the heat for a few more minutes until Caroline brushed her hands off.

"Is it done?" Christina asked, curious. For, of course, she had never triggered a geyser before and had no idea how this would work. "How long do we have to wait until it erupts?"

Caroline knelt and put her hand to her ear, as if listening for the answer to whisper out of the ground.

"Two minutes," she said.

"How do you know that?" Christina wondered.

Caroline shrugged. "It's noon so our powers get a boost."

"But why can't *I* tell?"

Caroline shrugged. "Maybe you're still too young. You'll get it one day."

Christina wasn't sure she would. She had watched her older sister her entire life and had discovered firsthand that Caroline had an inexplicable gift with fire. While all girls could create fire, Caroline seemed to have a very peculiar connection that Christina had never seen in any other girls. So she doubted that she would ever be as skilled with fire as Caroline no matter how old she was.

Caroline pulled a sloppy sandwich out of the pocket of her parka then laid it on the ground at her feet. Then she pulled the ring of rope off her shoulder and handed Christina one end. After that she walked to the other side of the area to the group of trees on that end and waved for Christina to walk to the other side. When the rope was lying flat across the surface of the soon-to-erupt geyser and the girls were hidden in the shadows of the trees, Caroline cupped her hands to her mouth and shouted, "HEY DAAAAAHM!!! COME GET YOUR SANDWICH!!!"

They waited several moments, but soon, like an animal lured into a trap, Dom came running into the area. He saw the sandwich sitting on the ground, but didn't notice the rope lying in front of it. He looked around for his sisters then stepped over the rope, swiped the sandwich off the ground, and brushed the snow off of it.

Then, with Dom's attention fixed on the sandwich, Caroline gave Christina a thumbs up and they both pulled the rope so it went taught. They swung it into Dom in one swift motion, sweeping his ankles and sending him toppling onto his backside. He landed clumsily onto the rock, cracking it under his weight, and the opening that resulted was just enough to release the heat that was bubbling underneath. To Caroline's delight, but very much Dom's horror, the geyser erupted with a towering blast of hot water that sent Dom shooting into the air, holding his backside with both hands. He landed nearly a hundred feet away, face flat in the snow, with his backside in the air and still sizzling.

Caroline and Christina burst into laughter then ran up to each other near the gushing water.

"Way to go, Chris," Caroline said, holding her hand out for their secret handshake.

Christina held her hand out and they bumped fists twice, made a flame between their palms, then smacked their hands together in a high five that extinguished the flame.

"He's gonna be so mad," Christina said.

"Well, he shouldn't have messed with us," Caroline replied.

Chapter six

The girls' celebration was short lived because, like most boys, Dom didn't appreciate having his backside burned by a geyser. In addition, like most boys, he promptly ran and told on his sisters to his mother.

"Why would you do that?" Mother scolded them when they were inside the igloo. Dom was laying on the floor flat on his stomach and Mother was gingerly rubbing a pouch of ice on his backside to cool his cheeks.

"He started it!" Caroline said.

"Did not!" Dom shouted.

"Did too!" Caroline shouted back.

"Enough!" Mother said, raising her hand.

There was a short silence as Mother went back to rubbing the ice on Dom's backside.

"He sprayed us with water, Mother," Christina added. "And he was making fun of us."

"So you *burned* him?" Mother said, squinting at her.

Christina looked at Caroline for help.

"What were we supposed to do?" Caroline replied. "Just sit back and let him push us around?"

Mother pinched the bridge of her nose and let out an aggravated sigh. "You don't burn your brother, girls. You know that fire is more dangerous than water."

"What?" Caroline scoffed. "So he's allowed to drown us, but we can't burn him?"

"You were in no danger of drowning, Caroline," Mother corrected her. "Stop being dramatic. Your brother, on the other hand, was in danger of losing his skin. Do you see what you've done to him?"

"But you didn't see what he did to us," Caroline argued. "Why doesn't he get punished? He should--"

"I don't want to hear it," Mother said, raising her hand for silence again. "Wait until your father hears about this tonight."

Caroline and Christina gasped, looked at each other, then turned back to Mother and exclaimed, "Father's coming home?!"

"Yes," Mother replied without looking at them. "He'll be home for dinner. And he won't be happy to hear what you've done to your brother."

But all of a sudden, Caroline and Christina were no longer upset. Father had been away for nearly a month working at the Imperial Palace. It was a three-day journey away, which meant that he could not travel back and forth after work each day and would remain away from home for weeks at a time. But tonight for dinner, they would see their father again and the joy of this event was enough to temporarily eclipse their frustration with Dom.

"Now hurry into the kitchen," Mother said to them. "I need help making dinner." She helped Dom to his feet and he held the pouch of ice to his backside as he stood. He walked away and stuck his tongue out at his sisters before leaving the room.

Chapter seven

That night the family had dinner together in the igloo. You may have never had dinner in an igloo so allow me to give you a brief description of what it was like. To begin with, the igloo itself was made of large blocks of densely packed snow and the walls rose in a domed curve all around. This packed snow was dense enough to withstand strong winds, but most importantly, keep heat in, thus warming everyone inside. Igloos could be relatively large, enough for nearly thirty people to sit in comfortably. But this igloo was the smallest in the village and only large enough to fit about ten people comfortably. There were also two levels inside the igloo--the lower level where the family members would crawl through the entrance and the upper level. These two levels were separated by a ramp of snow the family would walk up and down and the upper level was where most of the family activities took place. You may be curious as to why there was even a need for an upper and lower level. The reason, my dear friend, was simple. Cold air tends to fall while warm air tends to rise. Therefore, the upper level of the igloo was always much warmer than the lower level. This upper level, then, was where the girls and women slept and the lower level was where the boys and men slept and where the family normally had dinner. Speaking of which...

Dinner tonight was salmon, oysters, and jumbo shrimp. Since boys never got cold, they didn't care much about eating hot food even though Andromeno was always freezing. The girls would very much have liked grilled moose steak, but they had to eat whatever the boys and men wanted—even though the girls were the ones who were cooking it all—since, of course, they were the ones who could make fire.

Despite what Mother had warned, Father didn't seem to feel the least bit bothered by the girls' antics. As a matter of fact, he didn't seem to feel anything for the girls at all.

"How has school been?" Father asked Dom as he took a bite of his salmon.

"It's been so great!" said Dom, his mouth still full of shrimp. "I've been getting so much better at making ice, Father! I can't wait to show you! And today a boy at school thought he could make a bigger snow castle than me, but I made one and it was three times his size!"

"Well done, son," Father said, patting him on the back.

"We played tag," Christina announced. "And Cindy almost—"

Mother gave Christina a scolding look, but it was too late.

"You know the rules about talking at the table, Christina," Father said.

Christina lowered her head and frowned. "Only boys and men talk at the table."

"That's right," said Father. "Unless you're spoken to."

Christina nodded.

"And don't chew with your mouth open."

Christina shut her mouth then went back to poking her salmon with her wooden fork. But even though she went back to being quiet, she felt Caroline tensing up next to her.

"How are things in the Palace?" Dom asked, stuffing more shrimp into his mouth.

"Wonderful," Father said. "Emperor Andrew has big plans for the empire. He may not be the best emperor we've had, but he does have some good ideas."

Christina saw her mother roll her eyes, but she didn't say anything. Christina had learned how to read her mother's facial expressions so even in the silence, she knew that Mother was secretly making fun of Emperor Andrew. Mother hated him and thought that he was the dumbest emperor Andromeno had ever had.

"Like what?" asked Dom. "What's he gonna do? Is he gonna build another Imperial City? Is he gonna import new animals from other villages? Siberian tigers? Mooses? Is he gonna make another ice park?"

Father chuckled. "I can't tell you the plans yet, son. You'll find out soon."

"We missed you, Father," Caroline said boldly.

Despite the sincerity in her voice and despite the fact that she had said something quite endearing, it was met with a hostile frown from her father.

"What did we just say?" he asked her.

Caroline lowered her head and muttered, "Only boys and men talk at the table."

"Good," Father said. "Don't let it happen again."

With that, he and Dom went on talking about the politics of the empire while Mother and the girls sat and ate in silence. But after about twenty minutes of this, Caroline had had enough and she spoke up again—very loudly.

"It's not fair!" she shouted.

Father and Dom both snapped their heads in her direction and Mother gave her the same scolding face she had given Christina.

"It's not fair!" Caroline repeated. "Why do boys get to talk? Girls know things too."

"Like what?" Dom laughed. "Besides how to make really bad salmon?"

"Caroline!" Mother shouted.

"No," Father held his hand up. "I want to hear this."

"It's not fair that only boys get to do things," Caroline continued. "We can do everything boys can do. I wanna go to school. I wanna play with animals. I wanna play with you when you come home from work. And I wanna do more than just stay here with Mother and cook for you guys all day."

"Well, from what your mother tells me," Father replied. "You've been quite busy doing more than cooking all day. Did you think you were going to get away with burning your brother?"

Caroline swallowed nervously and the silence dragged on for several painful seconds. Mother kept scolding Caroline with her eyes. Cindy stared with shock on her face. Christina looked back and forth from Caroline to Father, wondering what would happen next.

Father wiped his mouth then folded his hands in front of his face. He did this every time he was preparing to say something very, very serious.

"Let me tell you something," he began. "You are a girl. Girls make fire. Andromeno is run by boys. Boys make water. Boys are stronger than girls. Because water is stronger than fire. End of story."

He lowered his hands and went back to eating his salmon.

But Caroline was not finished.

"That's *not* the end of the story!" she shouted. "What about the prophecy?"

"Don't you dare," Father threatened.

Caroline jumped to her feet and recited the words of the prophecy spoken hundreds of years ago:

'Today the empire's run
By boys who kill all the fun
But the frozen will fall
When the Chosen One calls
And then the kingdom will come.'

This was the prophecy. One day a Chosen One would bring everything back to the way it was in the beginning—the empire would be destroyed and the kingdom would be restored. But it had been so long that no one even remembered what the difference between an empire and a kingdom was. Furthermore, since the empire was where all the boys had the power, none of the boys liked hearing this prophecy. Which is why Dom spoke up next.

"That's a stupid prophecy!" he stood and screamed at Caroline. "And you're stupid for believing it!"

"Enough!" Father said. He motioned with his hand and Dom slowly sat back down. But Caroline stayed standing. "Caroline, everyone in the empire has a role. Boys rule and men give them advice. Women cook and girls keep quiet. Because water beats fire. End of story."

Caroline huffed angrily. "Well, if that's what you think, I don't wanna be a part of this story anymore!"

With that, Father said something Christina had never expected him to say to his own daughter. "We can't live without water. But we *can* live without fire. You can leave."

Caroline's eyes went wide in surprise. She looked at Mother, who said nothing, then back at Father, who just stared with an angry face.

Then Caroline shrieked at the top of her lungs, "I don't need you! I'm gonna show you that girls are better than boys! And one day, you'll all regret this!"

Then she turned and stormed out of the igloo and out of Christina's life.

A few seconds of silence went by and no one said a word. Christina wished that Mother had spoken up for Caroline, but she never spoke up for any of them.

Eventually, Father took another bite of salmon, told Dom something about the Emperor, and dinner went back to normal. But things were never normal for Christina after that. Because now that Caroline had left, she wasn't there to protect Christina from what happened later that night.

Chapter eight

After dinner, Christina helped Mother and Cindy clean the dishes outside while Father and Dom played with Ark, the pet sea lion, inside the igloo. Mother never said a word about what had happened and simply kept dipping the dishes into the water in the ice hole. The ice hole was a hole on the surface of the frozen river behind the village. They would fish there, wash their clothes there, and wash their dishes there. But Christina hated washing the dishes at night because the water was the coldest when it was dark. Even though Cindy was holding two balls of fire in her hands to give them light and keep them warm, they were all still shivering. But they had to wash the dishes at night because Father and Dom needed clean dishes for breakfast in the morning.

But even when the dishes were done being cleaned, Mother still hadn't said a word to Christina. When they went back inside, Christina finally decided that she was going to say something, but Dom ruined her chance.

"Hey, Tiny Tina!" he shouted and smacked her on her back.

"Owww!" Dom loved making his hand wet with icy cold water then smacking her back with it. "Leave me alone!"

"After you make me some dessert," Dom said. "I want an icee. Cherry with some strawberry swirl. Now go." He smacked her back again.

Christina winced and was about to go back outside to make the icee. But then she remembered what Caroline had said that afternoon: you either fight back or let them bully you. So in that moment, Christina decided it was time for her to fight back.

She turned to Dom, looked him in the eyes, and said, "You're not the boss of me. Don't tell me what to do."

Dom laughed, took a swig of water from his canteen, then stepped up closer and she saw that green glimmer flash across his eyes again.

"You think you can be tough now just cuz Carol left?" he said as he shoved her in her chest. "You're still just a little girl." He shoved her again and sprayed a line of water into her face.

Normally Christina would give in and do what Dom wanted, but not tonight. Not after seeing Caroline stand up for herself. So when Dom tried to shove her again, she grabbed his arm, screamed, and shoved him back. To her surprise, Dom screamed louder than she had ever heard him scream before. When she looked at him, she saw that he was holding his arm with his hand and staring down at it with a scared look on his face. His skin was red and sizzling.

"You burned me!" he shouted. "Why would you do that?"

Christina shook her head in disbelief. "It was an accident." Indeed it had been. She hadn't even realized that she had used her powers. But Dom didn't care and no amount of apologies would change his mind about revenge.

"You're gonna pay for that," he growled.

"No," Christina begged him. "Please. I'm sorry!"

But he grabbed her by her hood and dragged her out of the igloo and to the ice hole.

"Please no!" Christina screamed. "Mother, help!"

But no one heard her scream.

Dom grabbed her arms, lifted her up, then dunked her into the freezing water. The cold pierced her whole body and everything flashed white in her eyes. Then Dom pulled her back out of the water and she gasped for air. Then he dunked her back in the water again.

And again.

And again.

The fourth time that he dunked her, he dunked her too far and the water took Christina away, carrying her further down the river and under the ice.

Christina fought desperately as the water carried her away, banging against the ice above her. But it was no use. She couldn't hear. She couldn't breathe. She couldn't feel her body anymore. The water was so cold that it felt like she was swimming in knives. She was sure that she was going to drown.

Then, as if being trapped under ice wasn't scary enough, Christina suddenly saw a long dark shape swim towards her. The darkness was thick as a tree, but moved like water, as if someone had spilled a river of living black oil. It circled around her and its face hovered a few feet away from hers where two glowing green eyes stared at her. Beneath those glowing green eyes were two long white fangs. She had never seen this creature before, but from the legends she had heard, she knew immediately what it was: the Sea Serpent.

Its eyes glared at her without blinking, it flicked a green tongue at her, then whispered into her mind: *Chrissssstina.*

Now Christina was overwhelmed with not only the freezing water, but with the ice cold fear this creature was striking into her. She was also nearly out of air. It was at this point that the Serpent opened its jaws, which were wide enough to swallow her whole, and lunged for her. But then, just when it seemed that all hope was lost, the ice shattered above her and two hands reached down and pulled her out of the water.

She lay on the ice, shivering and whimpering from the cold, and she was shaking so much that she couldn't control it. She couldn't feel her body--not her fingers, not her toes, not even her chest. She tried to look up and see who had saved her, but suddenly, everything faded to black and she fainted.

Later, Christina woke up briefly in a cave near a fire. She could barely make out the shadow of a person sitting on the other side of the flames, but she was too weak to keep her eyes open. Then she fell back asleep.

The next morning, Christina was lying on the ground near the geyser her and Caroline had opened. Her clothes were dry and she wondered if they had been dried in the cave or from the warmth of the geyser. She didn't hang around too long to ponder, however, and realizing she was not far from her village, she made her way back home. But she never found out who had saved her.

That night changed Christina forever. See, most people are not born afraid of the things they are afraid of. Most people experience something terrible with a thing and then learn to be afraid of that thing. Many of the girls in

Andromeno hated water because boys beat them with it. But not many of them were afraid of it. However, because of what Dom had done, from that day forth, Christina became terrified of water.

But Christina also learned something else that night. Caroline had taught her that she had a choice to fight or be fought against. Now, because of what Dom had done, Christina had learned that it was better not to fight at all.

Chapter nine

The very next morning, Mother woke up Christina and Cindy to prepare breakfast. As usual, their job was to march to the ice hole and capture some fish. Unusually, however, Christina was no longer eager to visit the ice hole.

"What's the matter?" Mother asked when Christina didn't move from her bed on the floor.

Christina looked at the wall sheepishly. "I'm...I'm...I'm scared."

"Of what?" Mother scoffed. "The water?"

Christina slowly nodded her head. The memory of the Serpent flashed through her mind's eye and she shut her eyes. "There's...something in it..."

"Yes," Mother replied. "Fish. So go out and get it before your father and Dom get upset. You know how they are when they're hungry."

But Christina didn't move.

"Christina, get up this instant and go get some fish," Mother ordered her. "Why are you so scared all of a sudden?"

Christina struggled to force the words out. "Dom...he...last night...he tried to drown me."

Mother looked at her for a few seconds in silence. Then, just when it appeared that she was going to empathize with Christina's story, she scoffed and shook her head.

"If you want to be lazy, then just say so," she blurted. "Don't invent lies to get out of your chores." She turned to leave the sleeping quarters.

"I'm not lying," Christina told her.

"I'm supposed to believe that your brother tried to drown you?" Mother snapped, stopping at the top of the ramp. "Why would he do that, Christina?"

"Because I accidentally burned him."

"You burned him?!" Mother shrieked. "Christina, why would you do that?"

"It was an accident!"

"You know how dangerous fire can be! How many times do we have to tell you that you need to control yourself?"

Christina lowered her eyes.

Mother shook her head and marched down the ramp, leaving Christina alone with two things now: her fear of what Dom had done to her and her new shame from trying to tell her mother about it.

She never told anyone else what Dom did to her that night. Nor did she tell anyone about seeing the Sea Serpent. Mother didn't believe her and she knew that her father would say it was what she deserved. Either way, Christina wouldn't feel better and Dom would get away with it. She wanted so desperately to tell Caroline, but Caroline had never come back home after dinner. As a matter of fact, months went by and the family thought they would never see Caroline again. So Christina decided to forget about what Dom had done and pretended that it had never happened.

Chapter ten

Soon it was December and once again the family was preparing for the yearly pilgrimage to the Imperial City for the Rain Ceremony.

"Why do we have to go to the Imperial City every year?" Cindy asked her mother as they packed their bags.

"It's a pilgrimage, sweetie," Mother replied.

"What's a pig image?" asked Cindy.

"A pilgrimage," Mother repeated. "Is a very special trip where you go to a very special place."

"And it's *very* far," Christina added.

"And the Imperial City is the most special place in Andromeno," Mother said. "And the Imperial Palace is the most special place in the Imperial City. So once a year we go there to remember how special Andromeno is."

"Oh!" Cindy exclaimed. "That sounds fun!"

"Grab your bags, sweetie," Mother said, pointing to the tiniest bag on the ground.

"Are we gonna see Caroline there?" Cindy asked.

Mother stopped and stared at her for a second and Christina saw tears starting to well up in her eyes.

"Caroline is on a different pilgrimage," Christina jumped in. "So we might not see her this time."

Mother swallowed nervously and nodded.

"Time to go!" Father shouted from outside the igloo. "We're gonna miss the sled!"

So the family rushed out and followed him and Dom past the igloos and to the edge of the village where all the other families were waiting in groups.

You might be wondering at this point how people traveled around in an empire made of ice and snow. Well, the roads themselves were made of snow and most people rode giant sleds pulled by wolves. Then there were some boys who would snowboard, ski, or ice skate on special roads that were made of ice. Some boys would even swim in the rivers and lakes that weren't frozen. Other boys who were exceptionally skilled(mainly the Crystal Lords) would even make tracks of ice in the air that they would skate across through the empire over people's heads. But girls couldn't do any of those things because they couldn't control water. They weren't allowed to learn how to snowboard, ski, or ice skate either. So they had to wait for sleds whenever they wanted to go somewhere.

"Why do I have to get on this stupid sled?" Dom asked as they waited. "I can just skate my way there. I bet I can beat you guys. I'm faster than all these wolves."

"When you're thirteen, you can go on the pilgrimage by yourself," Father told him. "But for now, you go with us."

"Why do I have to wait a whole other year?" Dom scoffed. "I'm strong enough. You don't even have powers anymore, Dad."

Father squinted at him and let out one heavy breath. "You keep talking like that. One day your powers will be gone too."

It was true. None of the adults in Andromeno had powers. This was because as people got older their powers weakened until they were completely gone. On their eighteenth birthdays, boys lost the ability to control water and girls lost the ability to make fire. As a result, none of the leaders in the empire were grown-ups—all the most powerful people were boys who still had their powers. No one really knew why people's powers went away on their eighteenth birthdays. This was the way things were in Andromeno—boys had power and adults did not.

"All aboard!" Christina and her family jumped back as a giant sled slid in front of them pulled by twelve gray and white wolves. The wolves were as big as Christina was and grayer than the clouds in the sky. They turned their heads towards the families waiting and Christina and Cindy jumped back, afraid that they would bite. But Dom walked right up to them and confidently pet the wolves' heads.

"Get on, children," Father told them, walking around to the back of the sled.

You might have thought that there weren't that many animals in Andromeno since it was so cold, but you'd be wrong. There were plenty of animals, just not ones you would find anywhere else: like penguins, snow owls, arctic foxes, arctic wolves, polar bears, and seals. At school, every boy learned how to train every animal so they were masters at feeding penguins, swimming with seals, and hunting with wolves. Which is why Dom knew how to pet the wolves. But girls weren't allowed to learn because they weren't allowed to go to school. So the boys would train their pets to attack the girls to tease them. As a result, most girls were afraid of animals.

Christina and her family climbed into the sled and sat in the back as other families boarded the front rows. Once the sled was filled, the driver cracked his whip and the wolves lurched forward, dragging them along the snow faster and faster.

"How far away is the Imperial City?" Cindy asked.

"Three days, sweetie," Mother answered.

"Cindy watch out, a fox!" Dom suddenly screamed.

Cindy shrieked and jumped into Mother's lap. Christina grabbed Mother's arms and even some of the other girls in the sled jumped in surprise.

Dom threw his head back and laughed at the top of his lungs. "Scaredy cats!" He knew girls in Andromeno were afraid of animals and he loved teasing his sisters for it.

Eventually Cindy and the rest of the girls calmed down and Cindy went back to asking questions. Even though the family had been on pilgrimages before with her, she had been too young to remember any of the other ones. So she had a lot of questions.

"How big is the Imperial Palace? Can we go inside? And what do we do when we get there? Are there animals there? I don't wanna see any more animals."

Christina stared out at the scenery as her mother answered Cindy's questions. They had left the village of igloos behind and now there was nothing but white snow everywhere she looked.

"The Palace is bigger than any igloo you've ever seen," Mother explained to Cindy. "And no, we can't go inside. Only boys and men are allowed in there. When we get to the City we will all offer a sacrifice to Emperor Andrew. And yes there are animals in the City. But you'll be safe."

"What's a sacrifice?" Cindy asked.

"It's when you give someone something that's really important to you," Mother explained. Then she added, a little softer. "Even if you don't want to."

Cindy gasped. "Does that mean I have to give him my favorite blanket?"

Mother shook her head. "Emperor Andrew doesn't care about your blanket, Cindy. He wants food. So we saved up money all year so that we can buy him lots of food when we get to the Imperial City." Mother patted the bag she was holding in her lap.

"Ohhhh," Cindy said, patting the small bag on her own lap. "Does Emperor Andrew give us a sacrifice too?"

Mother smirked. "No, Cindy. We give him a sacrifice because he protected us the whole year. If we don't give it, then he might not protect us next year."

"Protect us?" Cindy squinted at her Mother. "Protect us from what?"

"Enough questions, Cindy," Father interrupted.

That was the end of the conversation.

At least for now.

Chapter eleven

Christina stared out at the snow around her as the sled kept moving. In the distance she could see the mountain range that formed a ring around the edge of the empire. Those mountains weren't as big or as special as the Crystal Mountain so they didn't have any special names. But the land behind the mountains did have a name—the tundra. The tundra was supposedly the coldest area of the empire. It was so cold, people said, that even the ground itself was frozen. No one lived there and no girl or woman had ever gone there. The only girls who'd ever gone there were the ones who lost the yearly challenges--and they never came back. But there were legends of boys who had been born in the tundra and grew up to become half human, half ice. They were called "Crystal Beasts". Christina didn't believe the legends, but she didn't ever want to go to the tundra to find out. She couldn't imagine how mean Crystal Beasts might be. Boys like Dom were mean enough.

The ride to the Imperial City was always very long and very boring and for the first three hours no one did anything but sleep. Since it's not very exciting to describe sleeping people, I'll take this time to share some more interesting facts about Andromeno with you.

Everyone in Andromeno wore different clothes depending on their age and their gender. Boys wore sleeveless blue tunics because their powers kept them from getting cold. If a boy was training to become a Crystal Lord, he would have a blue bandana around his head. Once he became a Crystal Lord, he would wear crystal rings on his fingers, a crystal necklace around his neck, and a crystal crown on his head. Crystal Lords were in charge of collecting taxes for the Emperor, fighting wars for the Emperor, and eventually one would be chosen to become the new Emperor. Not all boys became Crystal Lords, however—only the best and the brightest. But if you asked the girls, they would say only the maddest and meanest.

Speaking of girls, they wore thick, gray hooded coats called parkas that were made out of animal skin that kept them warm. The hoods had fur around them to keep the girls' heads and faces nice and toasty. They didn't wear gloves, however, since their hands were generally quite warm, being that this was where their fire would come from. You could imagine how difficult it was for girls who could make fire to live in a place that was so cold and unforgiving to fire. Sometimes the temperature was so cold the girls could watch their breath freeze before their very eyes. So they rarely ever took their parkas off and didn't spend too much time outside unless it was the middle of the day when the Sun was at its highest.

In contrast to the boys, all adults, men and women alike—who were boys and girls 18 years and older—wore thick fur coats that were usually black, gray, brown or white. Remember, adults lost their powers as they got older. So men could no longer get away with sleeveless tunics. Which was why Father always wore his thick coat. Mother, of course, wore hers for the same reason.

That's enough information for now. Let's get back to the story...

At about the fourth hour into the journey, the sled pulled up to a village and gave the wolves a chance to rest and drink some water. Meanwhile, the families climbed out and stretched their legs by walking through the village.

"Wake up, Tiny Tina!" Dom shouted. He held his hand over her head and a tiny waterfall poured out of his palm onto her face.

Christina gasped and coughed as she woke up and Dom ran away, laughing his head off.

Christina wiped her face and looked around at the village they were at. She was, of course, upset at Dom for doing that, but when she realized what village they were in, all her irritation melted away and was replaced with excitement. She recognized this village. This was where her cousins lived.

"Christina!" she heard someone shout.

She hopped off the sled and ran across the snow towards the igloos. Sure enough, her Uncle Harry and Aunt Leslie were standing outside one of them. Right next to them were two teenage twins: a boy in a dark blue sleeveless tunic with a hood and a girl in a dark gray parka.

"Joanna!" Christina shouted, running towards them. "Jonathan!" She reached them and threw herself onto both of them and they all hugged each other.

"How are things in your village?" Joanna asked.

"Same as always," Christina said. "Except Caroline is gone."

"I know," Joanna nodded. "I saw it in my flames."

"Really?" Christina asked. "When are you gonna teach *me* how to do that?"

"I can't, Christina," Joanna said. "But you'll learn other things."

Dom suddenly showed up behind the twins with his hands behind his back. "She ran away cuz she's being a baby."

The twins slipped away from him at the same time, as if they were afraid of being infected by his mere presence.

"I can see you haven't changed much, Dom," Joanna said.

"Oh you just wait," Dom replied. "Big changes are coming. You're looking at a future Crystal Lord. In the flesh." Then he pulled one hand from behind his back and held his canteen out towards Jonathan. "You look thirsty. You should have some nice cold water."

Jonathan didn't even look at the canteen. "No thanks."

Dom scoffed. "I forgot. You don't like cold water. Why do you like acting like a little girl?"

"And why do you like your water so cold?" Jonathan replied. "Oh that's right. It matches your heart."

Joanna laughed. "Burn!"

Dom spun his head in her direction. "You better show me some respect, Joannie. Or you might. Get. Bit!" Without warning, he pulled his other hand from behind his back and tossed a black snake at her.

She shrieked in shock as the snake landed on her arm and bit her hand. She grabbed it with her free hand and hurled it across the snow, trembling in fright. Before anyone else could react, Jonathan had already grabbed her hand, thrown his mouth onto the bite, and began sucking the venom out.

"Ill!" Dom cried. "What are you doing? You're not supposed to suck venom out of a snake bite. That's how *you* get poisoned too."

"What is wrong with you?" Jonathan spat at him.

"Relax!" Dom laughed. "It wasn't even *that* venomous. It's not a big deal."

"You know what else isn't a big deal?" Jonathan asked. He waved his hands at Dom's legs and a flurry of icicles shot through the waistline of his pants, slicing them on their way. Immediately, Dom's pants dropped to the ground, exposing his bare legs and underwear.

Joanna and Christina burst out laughing.

Jonathan pointed as he sang, "I see igloos, I see trees. I see Dom's ashy knees!"

The girls laughed even harder and Christina dropped onto her back as she roared. Dom, of course, didn't appreciate this one bit and pulled his pants up and hobbled away, crying to Mother that the twins were being mean to him.

"Thanks," Joanna said when they were done laughing.

"No biggie," Jonathan replied. He touched his lips and spat on the ground several times. "Tastes like copper. A lot better than Joanna's cooking."

"Whatever," Joanna rolled her eyes.

Christina loved her cousins. Jonathan was the only boy she knew who was nice to her and who would actually stand up for girls. He was also the only boy who wore a hood on his tunic because he wanted all the other boys to know that he was on the girls' side.

Joanna was the strangest of the two of them and seemed to have the ability to know things before they happened, which was why she had known that Caroline had run away.

Now, you may already know this, but even though twins look exactly the same, they are often very, very, different. This was certainly the case with Joanna and Jonathan. Joanna was very wise and patient, which was why she could tolerate Dom's antics. But Jonathan was much more abrasive and quick-tempered, which was why he was the one to cut Dom's pants off.

"We got you something," Joanna told Christina.

Jonathan handed her a royal blue pouch of animal skin tied at the mouth with a string.

"Happy belated birthday," the twins said together.

Christina gasped in delight. No one else in the family had even gotten her a birthday present. Quite frankly, she herself had forgotten that her birthday had passed. You can imagine that in a family where fathers kick their daughters out for simply speaking up at dinner not many birthdays would be celebrated. So Christina had gotten quite used to not receiving any presents. But her cousins had gotten her something--which was another reason she loved them so much.

"Thank you!" she exclaimed, hugging them both. She took the pouch, reached inside, and pulled out several tiny white pebbles. They looked like snow, but felt like ice. Christina wanted to be grateful for the unexpected birthday present, but was honestly confused.

"What is this?" she asked, trying not to sound disappointed.

"Salt," Jonathan replied with a grin.

Christina looked at him then at Joanna, expecting them to explain themselves.

Jonathan stepped closer to her and whispered in her ear, "It takes away boys' powers."

Christina gasped again. "Really?"

Jonathan nodded as he stepped back. "Salt makes it harder to freeze water so if you throw a handful of this at a Crystal Lord, no more ice for him until he takes a bath."

Christina looked down at the salt in her hand in awe.

"They can still shoot you with water," Jonathan shrugged. "But at least they won't be able to freeze you."

Christina scrunched her eyebrows as another question formed in her mind. "Why are you giving me this?"

"You'll find out soon," Jonathan winked at her.

"Are you ready for the pilgrimage?" Joanna asked.

"Yeah," Christina replied, still confused. "We have enough food and sacrifices."

"No," Joanna shook her head. "I mean are *you* ready, Christina?"

Christina squinted at her. "What do you mean?"

"This pilgrimage will be different than the others," Joanna told her. "Change is coming. Be ready."

Before Christina could ask any more questions, the sled driver screamed, "All aboard!" and it was time to leave. But Christina couldn't get Joanna's words out of her mind. What change was coming?

Chapter twelve

The sled rode on for the rest of the day with nothing more exciting to see than more miles of endless snow. Then, as the Sun made its descent and the horizon was turned to a blazing line of yellow fire, another line began to appear in the distance. But this line was actually *on* the snow.

"What's that?" Cindy asked her mother as she pointed at the approaching line.

"That's the border," Mother answered. "That separates our villages in the Outer ring from the villages in the Inner Ring."

Cindy scrunched her nose as she wondered why she had never seen any "rings" in her village. Well, of course, that was because the Outer Ring was not visible from the ground. If Cindy still had the ability to fly with wings of fire, like the girls hundreds of years before her, she would be able to soar thousands of feet into the air and see that the empire of Andromeno was a series of concentric circles. The outer circle, named the Outer Ring, was the largest of the rings and contained the poorest villages. The people there all lived in igloos. The next ring, the Inner Ring, was the second largest and contained villages that were a little better off than the ones in the Outer Ring. The people there lived in log cabins. Then there was the Crystal Lake which separated the Inner Ring from the Innermost Ring, or as everyone in the empire called it, the Imperial City. This was the smallest ring of all and mainly boys and men lived there in grand crystal mansions. Between each of these rings was a border. Why were there borders, you ask? You'll find out shortly.

The sled came to a stop in front of the line and Cindy was able to see firsthand that it was a giant wall of white ice nearly a hundred feet high. A long line of other sleds was waiting at an opening in the wall. By the time the sled Christina's family was on made it to the front of the line, the Sun was gone and the moon was hanging high above them in the night sky.

A group of three Crystal Lords stepped out of the gap in the wall and began circling the sled, inspecting it from top to bottom.

"How many girls in there?" one Crystal Lord asked.

"Twelve," one of them replied from the back of the sled.

"Twelve girls," the first Crystal Lord said, counting his fingers. "Twelve gold coins each. That's...one-hundred-forty-four gold coins to get through."

"What?!" the people on the sled protested.

"One-hundred-forty-four?!" cried one father. "That's outrageous."

"Twelve girls on a sled is outrageous," the Crystal Lord replied. "You pay up or you turn around."

"Why do we have to pay them, Mommy?" Cindy whispered.

"Because it costs money to travel from one ring of the empire to the next," Mother replied. "It's called a toll."

"But why do only the girls have to pay?"

"Because the empire charges taxes for having girls," Mother replied. "So we have to pay."

"It's not fair," Christina muttered. She remembered all the years before how Caroline had protested paying the daughter tax, much to the embarrassment of Father and Mother. But Christina would have preferred to have her older sister here than to go through the toll without her. Then, as she was thinking of what her sister would have done, another teenage girl in the back of the sled spoke up.

"And what if we don't want to pay?" she asked.

The sled went quiet as everyone tensed, waiting for the Crystal Lords to reply. The girl's parents scolded her and whispered for her to stay quiet.

"I mean, there are twelve of us and three of you," the girl went on, ignoring her parents' efforts to silence her.

The Crystal Lord who had announced the cost smirked. "So you're good at math. But you suck at astronomy. There's twelve of you, but one moon. So our powers get a boost. You wouldn't stand a chance."

The girl swallowed and the sled went quiet again. The parents put some of their coins together to pay the toll and handed them all to the driver who paid the Crystal Lords.

With that, the sled rode on into the Inner Ring without any more interruptions.

Chapter thirteen

The sled stopped shortly after to rest at the nearest village. Then the next day they carried on through the Inner Ring, stopping again every few hours to rest, eat, and to allow the wolves to drink. Finally, on the third day of traveling, they made it to the shore of the Crystal Lake, the lake that the Imperial City was built on.

Everyone climbed out of the sled and made their way towards the boats waiting at the dock. But when Christina saw the water, she stopped in her tracks and stood as still as a statue. Suddenly, she had a flashback of Dom dumping her in the ice hole. As if this wasn't terrifying enough, she was sure she heard the Sea Serpent's voice whispering from the water: *Chrissssstina.*

She shook her head and took several steps back towards the sled.

"Christina, where are you going?" Mother asked her, waving her to come.

But Christina kept shaking her head. "I don't wanna go."

"Come on," Mother insisted. "Stop being ridiculous. You've done this every year. Get on the boat."

Christina shook her head as she stared at the water, too terrified to move.

"Scaredy cat! Scaredy cat!" Dom teased, already inside one of the boats. "Tiny Tina's afraid of a little water!" Then he burst out laughing at the top of his lungs.

Finally, Mother walked over to Christina, grabbed her by her hand, and dragged her to the boat. Christina whimpered and tried to pull away, but Mother was stronger and before she knew it, they were on the boat and rowing towards the Imperial City.

"Scaredy cat! Scaredy cat!" Dom kept chanting.

Christina wrapped her arms around Mother's waist, buried her head into her coat, and shut her eyes, hoping that this would help her forget about the water and about Dom's teasing.

Finally, nearly an hour later, the boat made it to the center of the lake at the shore of the Imperial City and everyone climbed out. When they were on the shore, they found themselves in front of a pair of giant crystal gates that rose so high Cindy and Christina had to bend their necks back to see the tops. The gates opened on their own and everyone walked into the city where Christina and Cindy's jaws dropped at the sights inside. Even though Christina remembered what the city looked like, it was always amazing to see it every year. Do you remember how beautiful I told you the empire of Andromeno was? The Imperial City was where all of that beauty resided.

There were giant buildings of all shapes and sizes: some triangles, others squares, and others huge circles, and they were all made of ice. Furthermore, there were so many people. The crowds were so thick that Christina could barely see through the bodies. It was simply a moving sea of blue tunics and gray parkas. Boys were running between the adults' legs and throwing icicles at each other, grown men were arm wrestling at ice tables outside of stores, and women and girls were cooking over small fires scattered around the area. There were animals too. So many of them. There were wolf cubs chasing white tiger cubs, lines of penguins marching behind their trainers, sea lions bouncing leather balls on their noses while people applauded, and polar bears eating raw fish.

"Stay close, everyone," Father said as they walked through the crowd.

"There's so many people!" Cindy shouted. "Where did they come from?"

"Other villages," Mother replied. "In the other rings."

"Wow!" She couldn't help but twist this way and that as they walked, trying to see every possible thing in this new world. "Where are we going first?"

"We have to buy food for the sacrifices."

"LOOK!" Dom suddenly screamed. He dropped his bag and went running ahead of the family into a clearing in the crowd.

"Dom, wait!" Father yelled, picking Dom's bag up off the ground.

The family ran after him to see what was going on. When they caught up to him, they saw a group of teenage boys standing in a line with their fists to their chests and looking very, very mean. They all had crystal rings on their fingers, crystal necklaces on their necks, and crystal crowns on their heads.

"Crystal Lords!" Dom whispered.

Christina rolled her eyes.

The boys stomped their feet then clapped their hands in unison like they were performing a ritual. Then they started chanting as loud as they could, "Fire is danger, water is justice. Every girl's a stranger, so leave until it's just us!"

The crowd cheered as the boys chanted, but Christina didn't cheer. She didn't like this chant very much. As you saw at the previous Rain Ceremony, people in Andromeno said it all the time to remind everyone that boys were better than girls. Caroline would often respond with, "I'll show you danger!" and shoot a stream of fire at whoever was chanting it. But she wasn't here now and again Christina found herself sick to her stomach wishing she was.

The Crystal Lords kept chanting then started showing off their powers. They formed spiraling waterfalls over their heads, raised pillars of ice off the ground, then flipped off them and landed while a flurry of snowflakes rained down on them.

The crowd went wild and all the boys and men shouted the chant together, "Fire is danger. Water is justice! Fire is danger. Water is justice!"

Christina pulled on her mother's sleeve. "Can we leave now, please?"

Her mother looked down at her and nodded. "We will. But we—"

Before she could finish her sentence, a flaming arrow shot into the center of the crowd and stabbed the snow right in front of the Crystal Lords. The crowd stopped chanting and everyone stared at the arrow. Then another arrow landed. And another. And another. Until the Crystal Lords were surrounded by a circle of flaming arrows.

"What's happening?" Cindy asked, tugging on her mother's sleeve. Her mother lifted her up onto her shoulders so she could see.

Christina watched in suspense, waiting for what would happen next. The Crystal Lords stood up straight and looked around for where the arrows had come from. Then, out of nowhere, a group of girls came flipping through the air and landed in a circle around the boys. Christina's jaw dropped as she watched them all stand in unison. They were all wearing black parkas, black pants, and black boots and they had bright red masks on their faces.

"Who are they?" Christina asked her mother.

Her mother smiled proudly as she watched. "Rebels."

The Rebels picked up their flaming arrows from out of the ground, put them in their bows, then aimed them at the boys.

"Girls rule!" they shouted. "Boys drool! Fire's hot! Water's not!"

Then they fired the arrows at the Crystal Lords and thus began the most exciting fight Christina had ever seen in her life. The crowd went wild as the Crystal Lords and the Rebels fought, sending up bursts of water and ice and explosions of flames and fireballs.

The boys and men in the crowd cheered for the Crystal Lords, "Water! Water! Water!"

For the first time that day, Christina heard the women and the girls speak up too and they shouted, "Fire! Fire! Fire!"

"Drown 'em!" Dom shouted next to Christina. "Drown 'em all!"

The fight lasted several minutes, but Christina never took her eyes off the Rebels fighting. They were incredibly fast, incredibly skilled, and incredibly brave. But even though the Rebels fought hard, eventually, the Crystal Lords surrounded them and held giant balls of water over their heads, threatening to drop them onto them.

"Surrender, Rebels," one Crystal Lord said. "Water always beats fire."

The Rebels looked at the Crystal Lords and didn't back down.

Then one of them stepped forward and shook her head. "You win this round, boys. But we'll be back. Change is coming." Then she threw a tiny black ball on the ground and there was an explosion of smoke. The Crystal Lords dropped the balls of water and they splashed into the cloud of smoke. The crowd watched in silence, but when the smoke cleared, the Rebels were gone.

Chapter fourteen

Christina wanted to know where the Rebels had gone and who they were. She had so many questions. Were they good or bad? Were they stronger than the Crystal Lords? Could they be the ones who would change things? But Mother wouldn't answer her questions.

"We have to buy the food for the sacrifice," she told the family.

So off they went, through the crowd and towards the stands where food was being sold.

"Did you see that?" Dom was saying next to Christina. "The Crystal Lords were so cool! Those Rebels didn't stand a chance." He threw a flurry of icicles into the air and tried to mimic the moves the Crystal Lords had done. "Water always beats fire."

Father and Mother stopped in front of a man with buckets of ice lined around him with crabs inside.

"How much for one crab?" Father asked.

The man looked at Father then at Cindy and Christina. He chuckled as he rubbed his belly and made a face that Christina didn't like.

"Two hundred gold coins," the man said.

"What?!" Father shouted. "Two hundred?! Are you crazy?"

The man shrugged. "One hundred for the crabs. One hundred for the daughter tax."

"Would it help you to know," Father began. "That I kicked out one of my daughters this year?"

The man raised an eyebrow as if he were impressed. "Well, good for you. But the price is the same. Two hundred."

"I'll give you one hundred," Father offered, reaching into his bag.

The man laughed. "And I'll give you a black eye. The price is two hundred gold coins. That's it."

"No one in the entire empire sells a crab for two hundred gold coins! The standard price is fifty gold coins a crab, including daughter tax. That's the price in every village!"

"Well, we're not in a village, are we, mister? Welcome to the Imperial City."

Father stared at the man for a long time then finally turned his back and walked away with the rest of the family. See, Father was right. The regular price in every village for one crab was fifty gold coins. But in the Imperial City, the fishermen would make the prices as high as they wanted because they knew that people had to buy their fish and crabs for their sacrifices. It wasn't fair, but it was what they did and no one could do anything about it. Because if you didn't bring food for the sacrifice every year, bad things would happen to you. What sort of bad things, you ask? Oh, believe you me—you don't want to know.

Father went from stand to stand, asking more and more fishermen for better deals. But none of them were offering anything less than two hundred gold coins for one crab. Some even wanted more. Each time, Christina and the rest of the family followed close behind, silently hoping that one of the fishermen would treat them fairly.

While they were at one particular stand, Christina turned and saw the most splendid thing in all of the Imperial City—the Imperial Palace. It was just a stone's throw away from where they were standing and it was absolutely stunning. It was shaped like a giant triangle with tall towers rising and falling on both sides. It glimmered, glistened, and sparkled in the sunlight as if it were made of diamonds. If Christina stared at it too long, she was sure that she would go blind from the light bouncing off of it. Surrounding this spectacular array of crystal triangles was a ring of giant ice statues of the emperor, all facing outward, and standing with their hands on their hips, very majestically.

This was where Emperor Andrew lived. No one was allowed inside except for Crystal Lords and the older men who advised Emperor Andrew—and of course the men who worked in the Palace like Father. But no girls or women were ever, ever, ever allowed inside. (Except for the servant girls. But we'll see them later.) Christina would probably get in trouble for even looking at the Palace too long, which was why she eventually turned her eyes away and looked at the giant mountain behind the Palace.

The Crystal Mountain.

This was the highest mountain in all of Andromeno and the Crystal Lords had frozen it after the Flood. It was covered with snow and ice and was what kept the temperature so cold all the time. It was like a giant freezer in the center of the empire. It was so tall that Christina couldn't even see the top because it was covered by clouds. According to legend, the mountain was so cold that no one—not even boys—had ever been able to climb to the top without freezing to death. As if that weren't bad enough, there were allegedly wild beasts that lived on the mountain, beasts that were larger, more monstrous, and hungrier than any other beasts in the empire. Because of this, most people never dared to climb the

Crystal Mountain. Not many wanted to, anyway. After all, this mountain was what held the empire together.

"Please! Some food for a poor old woman!"

Christina heard a voice behind her and turned to see a woman begging in the street. She was dressed in dirty, torn, gray rags, and her hair was white and knotted under her hood. Her hands were bony with sagging skin, and she held them out to everyone who walked past her.

"Please," the woman pleaded. "Food for an old woman."

But no one paid her any mind. Everyone—men, boys, women, and girls—walked past her as if she didn't exist. Christina felt bad for her and wanted to do something. So she went back to Mother.

"Mother, can I give that woman some food?" she asked.

Mother looked at the old beggar then back at Christina. "Christina. We don't even have enough money for the sacrifice. We can't afford to help her."

Christina looked back at the beggar. She didn't understand why, but for some reason she couldn't look away. It wasn't fair. She had to help her. "Please, Mother? If it was you, wouldn't you want someone to feed you?"

Mother looked at the beggar again, sighed, then looked at Father, who was arguing with another fisherman. She quickly reached into her bag and gave Christina one silver coin. "This is all you get. Understand? Now hurry before your father sees you."

Christina took the silver coin and rushed to a stand selling warm soup. Boys and men didn't like warm things so soup was the cheapest dish to buy in the empire, even in the

Imperial City. So Christina bought a small bowl then ran over to the old beggar.

"Here you go, lady," she said, holding the bowl out.

The old beggar grinned down at Christina, revealing crooked yellow teeth. She took the bowl, lifted it to her lips, and drank it. But she never took her eyes off of Christina. Christina was amazed at how quickly she was drinking it—she must have been really hungry. But suddenly, the old beggar threw the bowl to the ground, grabbed Christina's face in her hands, and spoke directly to her.

"Today the empire's run by boys who kill all the fun. But the frozen will fall when the Chosen One calls. And then the kingdom will come."

Christina stared at the old beggar in shock, trying to pull away. But the beggar didn't let go. Then she uttered words that would change Christina's life from that moment forth.

"A daughter has been given. The Chosen One has come. All crimes will be forgiven. *You* are the Chosen One."

Christina's eyes went wide as the old beggar let go of her face and she jumped back.

"Go to the tundra," the old beggar said. "Your destiny awaits." Then, to Christina's utter amazement, there was a blaze of fire and the old beggar vanished.

Chapter fifteen

Christina never told her parents what the old beggar had said. They wouldn't believe her. After all, Mother hadn't believed her when Dom had nearly drowned her. She would most definitely not believe this. Worse yet, Mother and Father would probably get upset at her for thinking that she was the Chosen One. That was impossible. It had to be. But there was also something else that was just as intriguing to Christina. The beggar had disappeared in fire—just like the Rebels. But she was so old. How did she still have her powers? No women in the empire over 18 years old had powers anymore. It didn't make any sense. But soon, something else wouldn't make sense.

Christina and her family spent the next two days renting an igloo on the edge of the Imperial City. On the third day, Father finally managed to find a good deal on a crab and he and Mother burned it at the altar in front of the Imperial Palace. Afterwards they left quickly and didn't even stay for the Rain Ceremony. Christina wasn't sure why.

"You shouldn't have done that," Mother whispered to Father on the sled ride back.

Father didn't respond.

"I told you we should have simply left early and used the rent money to buy a crab," Mother said. "You know what could happen to us."

"They won't know who did it," Father whispered back.

Christina pretended not to be listening as she stared at the snow around her. But she *was* listening. Father had done something wrong. He had given a fake sacrifice because they didn't have enough money for a real one. Christina didn't know what he had sacrificed instead of crab, but whatever it was had Mother quite worried. Rightfully so because as I've told you before, when people gave the wrong sacrifice, bad things would happen. Very bad things.

But Christina kept her eyes fixed on the snow and said nothing. She stared at the mountains in the distance and remembered the old beggar's words: *Go to the tundra. Your destiny awaits.*

Christina shut her eyes. She couldn't go to the tundra. Even if she did believe this crazy old woman, no girl had ever gone to the tundra and come out alive. She would freeze to death and if not, she'd most likely get eaten by a pack of Crystal Beasts. It was better for her to stay home and pretend like it had never happened. But there are certain things in life that can never be ignored. Destiny is one of them.

Three days later, the family made it back to their village and unpacked in the igloo.

***

"I'm exhausted," Father said upon arriving home. "Let's have dinner."

"I want crabs!" Dom announced.

"No!" Father shouted. Then he stopped, gathered himself, and tried again. "No. No crabs. Make something else, honey. Anything else."

Mother nodded then turned to Christina. "Go get some fish."

Christina nodded, grabbed a fishing pole and a bucket, then left the igloo and went to the ice hole. It wasn't until she was a few feet away from the hole that she remembered what had happened there just a few months ago. Suddenly, she was having flashbacks of Dom dunking her in the water, her body started shaking, and she dropped the bucket in the snow.

"Come on, Christina," she tried to tell herself. "You can do this. You've done this before." But no matter how much she tried to convince herself, she couldn't take another step. See, even though Christina had been at the ice hole many times before without ever getting hurt, she couldn't remember those times now. All she could remember was the one time she *had* been hurt. Fear has a way of twisting our memories like that.

Because of this fear, Christina found herself sitting down in the snow and staring at the ice hole, trying to will herself to be brave, but failing miserably. Then finally, she gathered enough courage to step towards the ice hole and peered inside. Instantly, she heard a voice coming out of the water.

Chrissssstina.

She screamed and fell back onto her backside. It was the Sea Serpent.

With that realization, she decided that she could not do this. Not with the Serpent waiting for her down there.

Minutes turned to hours until finally it was nighttime, the moon was up, and she had no fish. What would Mother say? She decided that she would lie and tell her that the fish were all sleeping. So she got up and walked back to the igloo.

But when she was halfway there, she saw something that froze her in her tracks.

Crystal Lords.

A group of them skated across ice tracks in the air and landed outside her igloo. Without hesitation, one of them fashioned a giant hammer of ice the size of a moose that floated above his head. With one powerful swing, the hammer smashed through the igloo, knocking down nearly half of the wall. Now instead of a perfect dome, the igloo looked more like a cracked shell. The Crystal Lords rushed inside and Christina heard her mother scream.

"Did you think Emperor Andrew wouldn't notice?" a Crystal Lord shouted.

"Don't do this!" Christina heard Father scream. "Please, no!"

"Shrimp? You sacrificed shrimp instead of crabs?!"

"Please, leave my family alone."

"You know he's allergic to shrimp!"

"It wasn't us!" Father pleaded.

Christina dropped the empty bucket and ran to the igloo. She didn't have to crawl inside because the entrance had been destroyed. Instead, she crouched at the bottom of the ramp at the lower level and watched from behind a mound of snow. Her family had rushed to the upper level in an attempt to run away and the Crystal Lords were standing there with them. It was from this vantage point that Christina witnessed something she would never unsee. For as she watched from her hiding place, the Crystal Lords threw their hands out at Father and Mother and froze them into statues.

Christina's jaw dropped in disbelief.

"Noooo!" Cindy shouted.

A Crystal Lord turned to her and froze her too.

Christina covered her mouth in shock. Dom stood there in the middle of his frozen family and didn't say a word.

"Is there anyone else?" one of the Crystal Lords asked him.

At this moment, Christina realized that her life was in her brother's hands. It was also at this moment that she discovered how truly mean Dom was. Because at this moment, Dom snapped his head in her direction, pointed down at her, and announced, "My sister's over there!"

The Crystal Lords turned and saw her on the lower level.

"There she is!" they shouted, running after her.

Christina turned and rushed out of the igloo, sprinting as fast as she could. But she knew it would be no use. They could skate on the ice tracks and catch her in seconds. Or they could shoot her with ice from a distance. She was going to be frozen and there was nothing she could do about it.

Go to the tundra.

The tundra! That was it! The boys would never follow her there. She forced herself to run faster, farther from the igloo, past the ice hole, and towards the edge of the empire. She heard the Crystal Lords skating through the air behind her, but she didn't look back. She kept her eyes on the gray fog ahead of her and the mountains behind it. If she could make it through the fog and past the mountains, she'd be safe in the tundra. Just a few more feet.

Suddenly, a blast of ice crashed into the snow on her left. She screamed and nearly tripped and fell. Another blast of ice crashed on her right. They were getting closer. One more shot and she would be frozen. She was going as fast as she could, but it wouldn't be fast enough. They would have her soon.

"You froze my foot!" one of them shouted.

"No I didn't!" shouted the other. "You froze mine!"

Christina continued running, grateful for the glimmer of hope their clumsiness had afforded her.

"Get her!" she heard a Crystal Lord shout. "Before she gets to the tundra!"

More blasts of ice crashed all around her, barely missing her. Then, when she thought that she couldn't run anymore, she broke through the fog and fell flat on her face. Her nose hit the ground and she swallowed a mouthful of snow. But she forced herself back up and kept running deeper into the fog and through the mountains on either side of her.

"You're dead, little girl!" she heard a Crystal Lord scream behind her. "Have fun freezing to death!"

They weren't coming after her. She was safe in the tundra now.

But they were right. If she stayed here, she would surely freeze from the cold. So it seemed that the only way to survive was to stay here and die.

Chapter sixteen

Christina walked deeper and deeper into the tundra. The deeper she went the colder it got until finally she dropped to the ground and curled into a ball. She was too cold and too tired to keep going. But if you've ever been camping in the winter, you know how difficult it is to fall asleep in the cold. Christina would have very much loved to make a campfire, but there was no wood. Because in the tundra there are no trees.

So Christina was forced to lay on the frozen ground, shivering from head to toe. There is a point where you can get so cold that it becomes much more comfortable to simply let yourself freeze to death. This is the point that Christina soon found herself in. She eventually could no longer feel her nose. Or her fingers. Or her toes. But then, when she was sure that her legs were turning to ice, someone lifted her off the ground. She couldn't see who it was because her eyelids were almost frozen shut. But whoever this person was, their body was incredibly warm, as if there was a furnace burning inside of their chest. They carried Christina through the tundra and into a cave where they lay Christina on the ground and she finally fell asleep.

***

When Christina woke up, she was beside a fire of burning coals and her body was delightfully warm. She sat up and saw a hooded figure sitting on the other side of the fire.

"Did you know that you snore?" the person asked.

Christina didn't know what to say. "No. I didn't. But...did you save me?"

"No, child, I *ate* you."

Christina stared at the figure blankly.

"Of course I saved you, silly."

Christina laughed nervously. "Who are you?"

The figure reached up and pulled their hood away, revealing the person underneath. The old beggar. Christina gasped.

"It's you! The beggar from the Imperial City!"

"You really do enjoy pointing out the obvious, little girl." She handed Christina a cup of steaming hot tea and Christina gladly took it.

She was about to thank the old woman for it, but then smelled the unfamiliar, strange odor wafting from the cup. If you can imagine what a mixture of baby poop and tomato soup would smell like you'd have an idea of what this tea smelled like. Christina grimaced and nearly gave the cup back to the old woman, but knew that this would be rude.

"Sea buckthorn tea," the old woman told her, seeing her discomfort. "Trust me, it tastes much better than it smells."

Christina took a deep breath, lifted the cup to her lips, and took a sip. She was delighted to discover that the old woman was right--it did taste much better than it smelled, like a cup of warm oranges.

"Sea buckthorn berries grow where it's too cold for other plants to grow," the old woman explained. "Like the tundra. And they're quite good at keeping you from getting sick and weak. You'll need as much of it as you can get here."

"Thank you," Christina said. "And thank you for saving me. How could I ever repay you?"

"You could start by massaging my back," the old woman said. "You're a heavy little one. What do they feed you in that village?"

"My village," Christina said softly as she remembered her parents and Cindy. "The Crystal Lords...they froze my family." She felt the tears rising up behind her eyes, but forced them back down. Caroline wouldn't have cried. She would have sucked it up and kept moving forward. So that's what Christina was going to do. She would show no weakness. Just like Caroline.

"What are you doing?" the old woman asked.

"Nothing," Christina said, wiping her eyes. "I'm fine."

"I may be old, but I'm not stupid." The old woman moved closer to Christina. "If you're going to cry, then cry."

"I'm not," Christina said. "I'm fine. The Crystal Lords froze my parents because I was too scared to stop them. I'm not gonna be scared or weak ever again."

"Well, that's no fun. I was looking forward to scaring you."

Christina tightened her lips and stared straight into the fire, determined to not let one tear drop.

"Look at me, child," the old woman said.

Christina looked over at her.

"It's okay to cry. Crying is what makes us human. And sometimes crying can heal us."

Christina didn't say a word.

"But you can't heal what you don't reveal."

Christina kept her eyes on the fire and was determined not to cry. But the old woman's words were softening her heart and eventually,

Christina burst into tears and threw herself into her arms.

"There it is, child," said the old woman. "Let it all out."

Christina cried for what felt like hours and the old woman held her without saying a word. Then finally, she sat up, wiped her eyes, and said, "Thank you."

Christina looked around the cave and realized that it looked familiar.

"Wait," she said. "I've been here before. This is where I woke up after Dom dunked me in the ice hole. Was that you too? Did you save me?"

The old woman grinned.

Christina stood and suddenly her grief was replaced by curiosity.

"You saved me," she said. "You brought me here. You made a fire. I'm so confused."

"Most people would say thank you," the old woman said.

"You have powers," Christina added. "But you're so old."

The old woman stared at her. "And your parents are dead. Are you going to keep pointing out the obvious? Or are you going to start asking real questions?"

Christina opened her mouth to ask a question, but suddenly there was a bark and a small dog came running out of the shadows.

"What is that?!" Christina shrieked and ran to the farthest wall and tried to climb out of the cave. Obviously, this was foolish and she couldn't climb through the wall, but people often do foolish things when they're afraid. You may remember as well that every girl in Andromeno was afraid of animals because every animal in Andromeno was trained to attack girls.

"That is a dog, Christina," the old woman calmly replied. "His name is Fuji. And he won't hurt you."

"Tell that to him!" Christina cried, still struggling to climb the wall.

The dog was quite small, with fluffy gray fur and bright blue eyes, and was trying to sniff Christina's feet. But to Christina, it looked like a giant angry wolf with dripping fangs trying to bite off her legs. It's funny how differently things appear when we're afraid.

"Down, boy," the old woman said. At the command, Fuji quickly turned and trotted over to her, wagging his tail happily.

It took Christina a short while to gather the courage to come off the wall and to eventually come back to the fire. The dog was sitting quietly next to the old woman, but Christina made sure to keep her eyes on it as much as she could. Eventually, she was calm enough again to ask a question. "How do you still have powers?"

The old woman grinned again. "Do you know where your fire comes from?"

Christina nodded. "The Sun."

"No," the old woman shook her head. "That's a lie straight from the lips of the Sea Serpent."

Christina stared in surprise. That was what everyone in the empire had been taught their whole lives. Boys' powers came from the moon and girls' powers came from the Sun.

"Then where does it come from?" she asked the old woman.

The old woman grinned again, but this time there was a mischievous glint in her eyes. "Come. I'll show you." She stood and walked deeper into the cave, holding a flame in her hand to light the way.

Chapter seventeen

Christina followed the old woman through the cave into a tunnel then to a staircase that spiraled deeper and deeper underground. Fuji was with them too, which Christina wasn't happy about, but the old woman insisted that the dog had to come. Christina kept her hands on the wall to keep her balance and could feel the coldness from outside even through the rocks.

"Be careful, child," the old woman said in front of her. "Everything is downhill from here." Then she slipped and disappeared into the darkness.

"Watch out!" Christina shouted and ran after her. But to her surprise, there were no more steps, only a severely steep incline that shot almost straight down, and down Christina went, sliding on smooth rock on her bottom.

"Whooo hooo!" the old woman laughed beneath her. Fuji howled in excitement.

The rock slide carried Christina faster and deeper than she thought possible. But eventually, it leveled out slightly, so it was less steep and became more like a hill. Not only that, but it suddenly began to twist and turn in a downward spiral. It was at this point that it began to feel less like a danger to be afraid of and more like a ride to be enjoyed. So Christina laughed and threw her arms up as she went. It reminded her very much of bob sledding that the villagers would do down the snowy slopes. If you've ever gone bob sledding before, you can imagine just how delightful this giant underground slide was.

Finally, after what felt like forever, the slide leveled out completely and Christina slid onto flat ground then rolled to a stop.

"That was fun!" she said, jumping to her feet.

The old woman walked away and Christina followed her. They were in another cave, but this one was much, much larger than the one they had left behind. The walls were so tall and so dark that Christina couldn't see the ceiling and the ground was rough and rocky. It looked like they were inside a mountain. As they kept walking, Christina realized something strange. The cave wasn't cold. It was warm. *Very* warm, in fact. Furthermore, if she wasn't mistaken, she could see a bright red glow in the distance where the old woman was leading her to. They kept walking and made it to the edge of a cliff.

The old woman stopped and looked over her shoulder back at Christina.

"Come see," she invited her.

Christina stepped to the edge and her jaw dropped at what she saw. Beneath the cliff was a giant, boiling pool of red, liquid fire.

"A girls' fire doesn't come from the Sun," the old woman explained. "It comes from the Earth."

Christina stared at the pool of fire. She had never seen something like this before and she was so mesmerized by the sight of it that she didn't dare blink because she was afraid of missing even a moment of it. Fuji hopped to the edge and barked down at the fire and Christina briefly wondered what would happen if she kicked him over.

The old woman continued to explain. "At its core, the Earth is made of fire. In the same way, there's a fire inside of every girl. So as long as girls are connected to the Earth, they'll be connected to their fire. And this is why the first thing the Sea Serpent had the Crystal Lords do is freeze the Earth."

Christina had never heard anything like that before. A girl's fire came from the Earth? And that was why the empire was frozen? To keep girls from having too much fire? So many things made sense to her now. This was why her and Caroline never felt anything during the noon rituals. The Sun wasn't giving them power. Then she realized something more and looked at the old woman.

"That's why girls lose their powers when we get older!"

The old woman nodded.

"The longer we spend away from the Earth, the weaker our fire gets," Christina went on. "And it's why you still have your powers even though you're so old! You've been living here this whole time."

"Yes, child," the old woman groaned. "I'm old. We both can see that."

Christina was excited to be hearing this and even more excited that she was able to figure some of it out.

"Wait," she wondered. "If girls lose their powers when we get older because we're not connected to the Earth, why do boys lose their powers? They can still see the moon."

The old woman shrugged. "I wouldn't know. I'm not a boy."

Christina couldn't argue with that. But something else was also troubling her.

"Why are you showing me all this?" she asked the old woman.

"Haven't you been paying attention, child? Today the empire's run by boys who kill all the fun. But the frozen will fall when the Chosen One calls. And then the kingdom will come. You are the Chosen One."

"But how? I'm only nine years old."

The old woman turned and continued walking along the cliff as if she hadn't even heard Christina's question.

"I'm just a kid," Christina said, following her. But the old woman didn't reply and just kept walking.

"What am I supposed to do, anyway?" Christina asked her.

"Bring the kingdom back," the old woman said without stopping. "So that boys and girls can live together peacefully again."

"But what's a kingdom? And how do I bring it back?"

"You've seen the Crystal Mountain?" the old woman asked her as they walked into a stone room. She stopped in front of what looked like a long stone bed with a long object lying on top of it.

"Yes," Christina replied. "But what does the mountain have to do with anything?"

The old woman turned so that her back was facing the stone bed. "The Crystal Mountain is what keeps Andromeno cold. But it's also where the very first Crystal Lords trapped the king."

"Emperor Andrew?" Christina asked.

"No, child. There's a big difference between an emperor and a king. You'll discover that later. If the mountain melts, the empire will fall, the king will be freed, and the kingdom will come. Your job is to melt that mountain."

Christina looked up at the old woman then down at the ground. All of this was a lot for her to take in. Fire in the Earth. Being the Chosen One. Melting the Crystal Mountain. Then, as if the old woman was intent on overwhelming Christina with new discoveries, she turned to the stone bed, lifted the object off of it, and pulled out a glowing red sword.

"WHOA!" Christina shouted. You might think that Christina was surprised because the sword was glowing. But in reality, she was surprised because she had never seen a sword. Because, as you may have guessed, swords are made of metal and metal is forged in fire. Which means that most people in Andromeno had never made or even seen swords for the Crystal Lords would never allow girls to learn how to fashion weapons that could defeat them.

"What is that?" Christina asked.

"This is many things," the old woman said. "It's a weapon. It's a bridge. It's a messenger."

Christina stared at the glowing blade with her jaw hanging open in wonder.

"It can cut through almost anything. Anything but metal. And its fire never goes out."

"Wow," Christina breathed. "Is that what I have to use to melt the mountain? No. Is that to fight off Crystal Lords?"

"No, Christina. Boys are not the enemy. Neither are girls."

"Then who is?" Christina asked.

"The serpent. And you're going to kill it."

Christina looked up at that. "What?"

"The serpent. And you're going to kill it."

"But I've never even used something like this before!"

"I'll teach you."

Christina went back to staring at the glow of the sword.

"Hold it," the old woman handed it to Christina and she smiled from ear to ear as she held it by the hilt. Even Fuji's barking and panting weren't enough to distract her from this now. It was so beautiful to her.

"When you stab it into the ground," the old woman started to explain. "You can speak with the king. All you need to do is say, 'I ask for nothing more or less than this. To see my father, king of Vartanis.'"

Christina looked up at the old woman again. "My father? My father is dead."

The old woman grinned and the mischievous twinkle returned to her eyes. "You have much to learn, child."

Chapter eighteen

The next day, the old woman began Christina's training. She brought her outside and had her stand in the middle of the snow. Christina was wearing her parka and the old woman was wearing her hooded cloak, but Christina was shivering and the old woman was not.

"I'm cold," Christina said.

"You're in the tundra," the old woman replied. "Get used to it."

Christina rubbed her arms and shivered. "Don't you have a coat or something? I'm gonna freeze to death."

"Listen to me, Christina," the old woman said to her. "It's a cold world out there for a girl. The only way to survive is to make the fire inside of you hotter than the cold that's around you."

Christina kept rubbing her arms and shivering. That sounded well and good to her, but it did nothing to make her feel any warmer.

"How do I d-d-d-do that?" she said, her teeth chattering from the cold.

"There are four levels of fire," the old woman explained, pacing in front of Christina. "Each of them are a different color and each of them is hotter than the one before it. The first fire is red fire. All girls have red fire simply from being born as girls."

"Sounds g-g-good," Christina said. She desperately wanted the old woman to get to the part where this new fire would make her warmer. "What's the point?"

"Patience," the old woman said. "Each color fire can control the fire before it."

"What do you mean?"

"If your fire is hotter than someone else's fire, you can control their fire."

"Okay," Christina said.

"The first fire is red fire. The next fire is orange fire. If you have orange fire, you can control red fire."

"Sounds g-g-good," said Christina. "How do I get orange fire?"

"Orange fire is blocked by shame," the old woman continued. "And is released by acceptance." The old woman stopped pacing and faced Christina. "So I have one question for you: who are you?"

Christina looked up at her, still rubbing her arms. "I'm Christina. A poor girl from the Outer Ring."

"No," the old woman said. "Who *are* you?"

"Christina," Christina said again. "My parents are dead. So I'm an orphan. An orphan girl named Christina."

"No," said the old woman. "You're the Chosen One."

Christina shook her head. "But how? I'm just a little g-g-g-girl who gets beat up by her big brother and who was too s-s-s-s-scared to protect her parents."

"That doesn't change anything."

"The Chosen One is supposed to help boys and girls live together. How am I the Chosen One if I couldn't even protect my parents?"

"You *are* the Chosen One!" the old woman repeated.

"I let them die!" Christina shouted. She was sure that she would have cried, but her tears seemed to be frozen on her face. She stared at her feet and sniffled as she shivered. "My parents are dead. And it's all my fault."

The old woman stared back at her in silence for a few moments. For those few moments, the only sound in the tundra was the chattering of Christina's teeth.

"Take out your sword," the old woman eventually said.

Christina reluctantly reached into the scabbard on her back and drew her sword.

"Stab it into the ground," the old woman told her.

Christina stabbed it into the ground.

"Now say the spell," said the old woman.

"I don't want to," Christina grumbled.

"Say the spell," the old woman repeated.

Christina sighed then recited the spell. "I ask for nothing more or less than this. To see my father, king of Vartanis."

There was a swirl of red fire around the sword and suddenly the head of a man wearing a blazing crown appeared in the flames. Christina fell on her backside in the snow and stared at the head in the fire in shock. She was quite surprised by the sight, but was also very grateful because this head of fire was incredibly warm. She no longer had to rub her arms and her teeth were no longer chattering.

"Christina," the head in the fire said. "My name is King Christopher. And you are my daughter."

Christina stared at him and shook her head. "Your daughter? That's impossible. My father got killed by the Crystal Lords."

"Well," King Christopher smiled gently. "Let me explain. My great-great-great-great-great-grandson was your father. So you, Christina, come from a king. Which makes you a princess."

Christina stared at King Christopher in silence. It was quite a lot for her to take in.

"What's a princess?" she asked.

King Christopher chuckled. "A princess is a girl who has power, but doesn't know how to use it yet."

Christina thought that over for a second.

"You have power, Christina," King Christopher said. "Because whether you like it or not or believe it or not, you are the Chosen One."

Christina looked away at that, still struggling to accept the truth. Of course, it sounded much more exciting coming from a flaming head. But she still felt unworthy. How could she be this great hero everyone was waiting for when she had allowed something so terrible to happen?

"Christina," King Christopher said. His voice seemed to breathe warmth into her and she sighed with content. "We all make mistakes. We all fail. But we are more than our mistakes and our failures. You are the Chosen One. And nothing you do or fail to do will ever change that."

Then, with a swirl of flames, the fire vanished and King Christopher was gone. Christina sat in the snow and started shivering again as the cold returned to her.

The old woman walked up to her.

"You can't change what happened," she said. "But what happened can change you. You can keep beating yourself up or you can get up and make sure the Crystal Lords can never do this again."

Christina took a deep breath as she thought the woman's words over. Then she stood to her feet and returned her sword into her scabbard.

Then, without warning, the old woman shot a blast of red fire into Christina's chest. Christina yelped and jumped back from the burn. She hadn't realized that fire could still burn her. That genuinely hurt. Why was the old woman doing this?

"Who are you?" the old woman asked.

"I'm Christina," Christina replied.

The old woman blasted her again and Christina yelped again. "Weren't you listening? You know who you are. But until you accept it, your orange fire won't burn. So who are you?"

Christina looked down at the ground and answered softly, "The Chosen One."

"I can't hear you!" the old woman said then she blasted her again. "Who are you?"

"The Chosen One!" Christina shouted.

"Who are you?!" the old woman shouted back. Then she sent the biggest blast of fire of the day at Christina.

But when the fire came, something new was burning inside of Christina and she shouted at the top of her lungs, "I am the Chosen One!" As she did, a burst of orange fire exploded from her body. The red fire came to a stop in front of her without touching her and with a wave of her hands, it curled back around away from her.

The old woman smiled. "Well done."

Chapter nineteen

For the next three months, the old woman(who Christina nicknamed "Nana") taught Christina how to use orange fire. Christina fought with orange fire, cooked with orange fire, and warmed herself with orange fire. Then, when she thought she'd exhausted everything she could do with orange fire, Nana showed her another unexpected way of using it...

"Burn me!" Nana shouted, tossing orange flames at Christina.

Christina sprinted away as the flames singed the snow on her heels. She ran a half circle around Nana before screaming and sending a blast of orange fire at her back.

Nana saw it coming and spun in time to curl the blast away from her.

The two faced each other as the smoke cleared and Nana grinned as a single flame flickered on her shoulder.

"Again," she told Christina.

Christina groaned and dropped her arms to her sides. "But I've done it a hundred times."

"It has to be perfect."

"But isn't it okay not to be perfect sometimes?"

Nana didn't miss a beat. "No. Water beats fire. Which means that you have to be twice as strong as any boy. Twice as fast as any boy. Twice as smart as any boy. Being perfect isn't an option. It's the only way to survive."

Christina sighed, but she knew there was no point in arguing. So she lifted her hands again and formed flames in her palms.

"Again," Nana told her.

On and on they went until Christina was able to land flames on her for five straight rounds.

"Well done," Nana told her.

Christina grinned, breathing heavily as she stood there. It had taken her hours of fighting, but she had finally consistently done it. She should have been proud and yet, she still felt unsettled.

"Come inside," Nana said as she walked past. "It's time for dinner."

But Christina didn't move.

"Don't tell me you're not hungry."

Christina looked down at her hands, still glowing red from the fire she had been shooting all day. "Something's bothering me, Nana."

Nana folded her hands in front of her as she listened.

Christina was still looking at her hands. "I'm getting better and better every day. But I still feel like I'm not good enough."

"There's always room for improvement," Nana agreed. "And that's why I'm here."

"No," Christina shook her head. "I'm not talking about my fire." She lowered her hands and looked towards the mountains in the distance. She wasn't sure, but she was fairly certain that was the direction of her home village. "I mean...all the times I wasn't good enough in the past. Like...being good enough to help Caroline. Maybe she would've stayed if I had been better."

Nana watched her silently for several moments. "Come inside. There's something else you need to learn."

When they made it back to the cave, Nana had Christina sit at the base of a fire in the center and began the unexpected lesson on what else orange fire could do.

"Sit still," she told her.

Christina followed her instructions. But just when she was getting settled, Fuji walked over and licked her face.

"Uggggh!" she cried, wiping her cheek.

He was much, much bigger now. Big enough that she could nearly ride on his back. But even after a year of living with him, she was still getting used to him. She was no longer afraid of him, but wasn't quite sure she liked him yet.

"Down, boy," Nana ordered him and he walked to her side.

Christina sat with her legs crossed and her hands in her lap.

"I'm going to teach you how to simmer."

"Simmer what? Soup?"

"No. Truth."

"What?"

"Stop asking so many questions," Nana scolded her. "Now close your eyes."

Christina obeyed.

"Remember that I taught you that each level of fire is stronger than the first?" Nana asked her.

"Yes."

"And each level can control the level that comes before it?"

"Yes."

"Your orange fire was blocked by shame and was released by acceptance. But there's still shame in you. Your orange fire can help you master it."

"How?"

"That's what I'm teaching you, child," Nana scolded her. "Pay attention. Make a ball of red fire."

Christina obeyed and formed a floating ball of red fire in her hands above her lap then looked over at Nana. "Now what?"

"Who's giving the instructions here?"

"Sorry."

"And close your eyes."

"Sorry."

"Now, think of the things you're ashamed of."

Christina kept her eyes shut as she took a deep breath and recalled the things she felt ashamed of. She recalled Caroline scolding her for not standing up to Dom with her.

Why didn't I do something? she thought to herself. *I should've helped. I should've thrown a fireball at Dom's head or something.*

She recalled the night at dinner when Caroline stood up to Father and he threw her out. *Why didn't I do something then? I just sat there. I should've said something. I should've told Mother to say something. I should've run after Caroline. I should've gone with her!*

She recalled the night the Crystal Lords came and froze her parents and Cindy. This time she didn't have to ask herself why she hadn't done something. *I wasn't brave enough. They're dead because of me.*

Then, as if Nana could read her mind, she interrupted Christina's thoughts with, "If you're thinking it was all your fault...it probably wasn't."

Christina sniffled and bit her lip to keep herself from crying.

"But even if it was, there's nothing you can do about it now," Nana continued. "Beating yourself up for the things you didn't do won't change the fact that you didn't do them."

"So what do I do?" Christina asked her.

"Who's giving the instructions here?"

"Sorry."

"And close your eyes."

"Sorry."

"Accept it," Nana went on. "Stop trying to change it. It happened. And you're here because it happened. So accept it and let it go."

Christina kept her eyes closed as she went through her memories again.

"You're still good enough," Nana told her.

Christina saw herself standing there while Dom splashed Caroline.

"I'm still good enough," she told herself.

She saw herself sitting at the table while Caroline stormed out of the igloo.

"I'm still good enough."

She saw herself hiding as the Crystal Lords froze her family.

"I'm still..." she sniffled before pushing the words out. "I'm still good enough."

When she had said the words the third time, she felt a warmth rise inside of her, like a soft blaze of acceptance had swelled in her heart. A tear rolled down her cheek and she breathed a heavy sigh of relief.

"Open your eyes," Nana told her.

When she did, she saw that the fire in her hands had turned from red to orange.

Nana placed her hand on her shoulder. "You're still good enough. And when you forget, simmer to remember."

Christina nodded then reached up and hugged her neck.

Chapter twenty

Christina continued training with orange fire for the rest of the year, adding her new ability to simmer into the mix. Then, after a year's worth of fighting, cooking, warming, and simmering, she had mastered orange fire and was ready to move on to the next level.

One morning, Nana brought Christina to a hill overlooking a low valley of gray stone. The hill was snowy, but the valley was simply stone. But from where they were sitting on the hill, it was difficult to tell if it was really stone or if it was frozen.

"What are we doing here?" Christina asked. She wasn't shivering as much today as she had been a year ago. The orange fire burning inside her was helping keep her warm. Fuji licked Christina's ear and she pushed him away. He had grown to the point where his head was level with hers. She still wasn't the biggest fan of dogs and the fact that he kept getting bigger didn't help ease her discomfort.

"The next level of fire is white fire," Nana explained. "White fire is blocked by bitterness and is released by forgiveness."

"Cool," Christina said. "Bring it on. What do I do?"

Nana made a series of signs with her fingers and Christina stared at her blankly.

"I don't speak sign language," Christina said.

"Well," Nana said. "We'll have to change that, won't we?" Then she pointed down into the valley and Christina watched as a creature emerged from behind a pile of boulders. It must have been sleeping behind them at first because she hadn't noticed it there before. Now that she had noticed it, she wished she hadn't because it was quite a gruesome-looking creature. Half of its body was completely frozen in jagged ice and the other half was pale skin. The ice half was unmistakably larger than the skin half, making its body horribly misshapen so that one shoulder was at least a foot higher than the other, its back was a giant hump, and one arm was twice the size of the other. But its face was where the monstrosity was clearest. One side was completely covered in sharp, piercing icicles with one gaping black hole where an eye should have been and the other half was the normal fleshly face of a young boy.

"What is that?" Christina asked.

"A Crystal Beast," Nana explained. "Its ice is so thick and so cold that red fire and orange fire aren't hot enough to melt it. Only white fire can break through."

"Alright," Christina rubbed her hands together. "Let's do this."

"But your white fire will only be released if you forgive your brother."

"Got it!" Christina said. But she really didn't have any idea what she was saying. She simply wanted a chance to use her fire in a fight. She had never fought anyone with her fire yet and she was itching to test her powers out. If she had waited just a little longer, she would have heard Nana explain just how exactly she was supposed to forgive her brother. But she didn't. Instead, she slid down the snowy hill and rushed straight towards the Crystal Beast.

"Hey, Ice Breath!" she shouted. "Name's Christina!"

The Crystal Beast grunted as it turned to her.

"Is it hot out here or is it just me?" Christina asked it. Then she rubbed her hands together, shut her eyes, and said, "I forgive Dom for all the stupid stuff he did to me." Then she opened her eyes and threw a fireball at the Crystal Beast. She expected the fire to come out white, but instead, it was orange. The fireball hit the Crystal Beast's head and fizzled out instantly.

There was a beat of silence as the beast rubbed its head then looked at Christina. Then it roared and charged her.

"Uh-oh," Christina whispered.

She turned to run, but the Crystal Beast was much quicker than she had expected and blocked her at the foot of the hill. She fired a flurry of orange fireballs at it, but they did nothing. Soon the Crystal Beast was in her face, punching her with its giant, frozen fist, and knocking her this way and that. It only took a few solid blows to the head before Christina dropped to the frozen ground and everything went black.

Chapter twenty-one

Christina woke up in the cave again next to a warm fire.

"As I was saying," Nana said. "You have to forgive your brother for everything he's done. Then you'll release your white fire. And then you'll be able to defeat the Crystal Beast."

Christina sat up and rubbed her head. "Sorry. Maybe I should have let you finish."

Fuji ran up to her, panting and ready to lick her, but she moved away from him.

"But why should I forgive my brother?" Christina asked. "What he did was wrong. He bullied me. He called me names. He almost drowned me."

"Forgiving someone doesn't mean that what they did was right," Nana explained. "It means that you're not going to get revenge."

Christina looked into the fire and thought about that for a moment. She remembered the times Dom had pushed her and her sisters around and all the names he had called her.

"I don't want to forgive him," she said. "He doesn't deserve it." Then she opened her hand and made an orange fireball in it. "I'm stronger now. I can fight back. And I want him to pay for what he did."

The old woman walked over to Christina and stood in front of her. "I know you think that will make things better. But it won't. Bitterness will make you cold." She reached down and closed Christina's hand and the fireball vanished. "Which will eventually put your fire out."

Christina looked up at her.

"In other words," Nana continued. "Forgiveness isn't for your brother, it's for you."

Christina looked down at her now empty hand. She remembered all the times Dom had pushed her around. All the times he'd called her mean names. All the times he'd made her cry. She remembered when he had dunked her in the ice hole. Most of all, she remembered how he had made the Crystal Lords chase her into the tundra. She wanted to be angry at him and now that she was stronger, she wanted to get him back. He deserved it. She wanted to give him a mouthful of fireballs and burn his throat from the inside out.

"But I'm the Chosen One," Christina chuckled. "Can't I get away with not forgiving him? I mean, don't I get some kind of special privilege?"

Nana scoffed. "I can give you a special beating if you'd like."

"No that's okay," Christina shook her head. "But seriously…isn't there a way around this?"

"You asked me what the difference was between an empire and a kingdom," Nana replied. "An empire is grown through conquests. A kingdom is grown through relationships. But there can be no relationships without forgiveness. If you can't forgive your brother, then you can't bring the kingdom."

Christina sighed heavily. It was difficult to argue when Nana explained it in such uncertain terms. But Christina knew she was right. How could she be the Chosen One and lead boys and girls to work together if she couldn't forgive her own brother? Burning Dom's insides wouldn't bring Mother and Father back. It wouldn't bring Cindy or

Caroline back. It certainly wouldn't bring the kingdom back. What's more, as Christina sat there, Nana's words came back to her: *Boys aren't the enemy. The Serpent is.* Then Christina wondered: what if Dom was only mean because he didn't know any better?

She breathed a great sigh then said words she never thought she would say out loud.

"Dom, I forgive you."

"For what?" Nana asked.

Christina sighed again, this time with much more irritation. "For bullying me. For calling me 'Tiny Tina'. For letting the Crystal Lords freeze our family. For making the Crystal Lords chase me. And for…dunking me in the ice hole."

When she finished saying those words, she felt a warmth grow inside of her. It swelled from her belly up to her chest then spilled over through the inside of her arms.

"I think I feel it," she told Nana.

Nana made a series of signs with her fingers at her.

"Why are you doing that?" Christina said. "I told you, I don't understand sign language."

"Well," Nana replied. "We'll have to change that, won't we?"

"Okay…" Christina said, still confused by her. "What do I do now?"

"Get up there," Nana told her. "And finish the job."

In just a few short minutes, they were both back out on the hill overlooking the Crystal Beast's den and watching it chew on a boulder. Christina slid down the hill and landed behind the beast. It turned then stood as it growled down at her. Christina took a deep breath as she looked back at it.

This time when she looked at it, she saw something she hadn't seen before. The human side of the Crystal Beast had a slight resemblance of her brother. Normally since she hated her brother, this would cause her to hate this beast even more. But now that she had forgiven her brother, a beast who looked like him made her feel something unexpected—compassion.

The Crystal Beast roared and marched towards her. Christina took a deep breath, held her hand out, and released a burst of fire at it. To her delight, the fire came out blazing white. Furthermore, instead of being a great, wild blaze like her red and orange fires, this white fire came out in a thin, controlled stream, like a spear of flame shooting from her hand. The fire hit the Crystal Beast's frozen side and it stopped running instantly. Christina held the spear of fire steady on its body and watched as little by little the ice melted. The Crystal Beast looked down at its body in surprise. Now instead of a giant, brutish, misshapen beast, a small pale-skinned boy stood in front of Christina.

He looked at her in confusion then back down at his skin and pants. Then he looked back up at Christina and said two words: "Tank...you."

Christina was too surprised to say anything in return and watched as the boy turned his back on her and walked away, up the hill, and disappeared in the distance.

Chapter twenty-two

While Christina was enduring the harsh realities of training in the tundra, Jonathan was enjoying the thrill of boyish games in his village. The particular game he was playing on this night involved one team of boys trying to carry a rather large snowball from one end of the playing field to the other without being stopped by the opposing team. The rules were simple: the team with the snowball could carry it to the other side in any way possible, the opposing team could stop the snowball from being carried in any way possible, and the snowball had to remain intact at all times or it would be forfeited to the opposing team. The game was aptly called "Snowball". The boys were not very clever at naming things.

"Over here!" one of Jonathan's teammates called to him as he sprinted across the snow.

Jonathan cradled the snowball in his arm as he weaved in between boys trying to grab him. They raised pillars of snow around him to block his path, but he raised a pillar of snow of his own that launched him over their pillars.

"I got him!" a boy on the other team shouted as he ran towards the falling Jonathan. He rushed underneath Jonathan and caught him in his arms.

"Oh, Darius," Jonathan said, imitating a girl's voice. "You're so big and strong."

Darius dropped him in the snow and was shocked that the snowball wasn't in Jonathan's hands. For while falling through the air, Jonathan had managed to pass it to his teammate Fred, who was already on his way to the goal.

"Get him!" Darius ordered his teammates.

He and the three other boys on his team rushed after Fred and sent blasts of snow after him, trying to knock him to the ground. Darius formed a wave of snow beneath his own feet and surfed it as he sped after Fred. It seemed that within seconds Darius would be upon him. However, just as Darius was reaching out to grab Fred's shoulder, his wave of snow turned to a wave of glistening ice and he skated wildly out of control, tumbled off, and landed face flat in the snow.

"That looked like it hurt," Jonathan laughed as he smoothly skated past on his own sheet of ice.

"Not fair!" cried another boy named Darion. "Jonathan can phase shift!"

The next moment, Fred crossed the goal line and smashed the snowball on the ground in victory. The team gathered around and cheered as Darius' team recovered.

"Five to three," Jonathan announced. "One more point and we win."

Darius limped over with two of his teammates holding him up on either side.

"What happened?" Jonathan asked.

"You happened," Darius scoffed. "I slipped on your ice and twisted my ankle."

"I told you we shouldn't let him phase shift!" Darion complained. "None of us can do that yet."

Allow me to enlighten you on what Darion meant by this. You may well know that water exists in many phases, including liquid and solid. All boys were born with the ability to control water in any of its phases, but they could not shift it from one phase to another. This required an extraordinary degree of skill and the only boys in the empire able to accomplish this feat were Crystal Lords--and of course, Jonathan.

"It's not our fault you're still a buncha snowflakes," Fred laughed.

Jonathan held his hand up to stop him. "Relax, Fred." He looked at Darius. "Sorry about that. Didn't mean to hurt you."

"No worries," Darius shrugged. "I'll just sit the rest of the game out."

"But now it's uneven!" shouted Darion. "It's four against three! And Jonathan is basically a Crystal Lord! I'm not playing anymore."

"Stop being such a girl!" Fred teased.

"I'm not a girl!" Darion cried.

Jonathan looked around and noticed Joanna in the distance just outside their igloo. She was sitting cross legged near a wood fire and holding a ball of orange fire in her hands.

"Speaking of girls..." he said to himself. Then he jogged over as he called out to her. "Hey, Jo! You wanna play with us?"

The boys all looked at each other in disbelief.

"Is he doing what I think he's doing?" Darion asked Darius.

"He better not be," Darius muttered.

Much to their dismay, a few moments later, Jonathan came running back with Joanna trailing close behind.

"You got a new player," he announced. "Darius can't play because he has glass ankles, we don't wanna sit around here watching the snow grow, sooooo Joanna can take his place."

The boys all looked at each other in a second of silence then suddenly burst out laughing.

"She's a girl," Darius said, catching his breath. "She can't play Snowball. She'll get hurt."

"That didn't stop *you*, Twinkle Feet," Jonathan countered.

Darius narrowed his eyes at him.

"That's different, Jonathan," Fred said. "She can't even control water. She's literally gonna be useless on their team and she's not gonna be a challenge for us. We can just throw some snow on her and she'll be out of the game."

"She's a lot better than you think," Jonathan argued. "Give her a chance. Guys, you just said I'm like a Crystal Lord. She's basically a Rebel. I bet she can beat any of you guys in a fight."

The boys scoffed.

"She's not playing," Darius announced. "This is Andromeno, Jonathan. Not some...some...stupid girls club."

Jonathan tapped his chin at that. "Hmmm. So, what I'm hearing is you're too scared you'll get beat by a girl."

The boys gasped. Darius tried to step up to Jonathan, but apparently forgot that he was injured and nearly toppled forward. His teammates adjusted his arms on their shoulders then helped him move up to Jonathan.

"No matter what you say, no matter what you think, girls will never be better than boys," he hissed.

"You're right," Jonathan nodded. "No point in saying or thinking. How about doing?"

Darius raised an eyebrow curiously.

"I challenge any of you," Jonathan offered. "If you beat me, then I'll leave and the teams will be even again. But if I beat you, then Joanna plays."

Joanna had been quietly watching this entire time, but as things had gotten much more hostile she became much more uncomfortable.

Now, at her brother's offer of a Challenge, she felt compelled to intervene.

"Jonathan," she whispered to him. "Really, it's not a big deal. I don't have to play."

Jonathan turned to her. "You're better than them and you know that. I know that. Now it's time for them to know that." He turned to the rest of the boys. "So what's it gonna be, snowflakes?"

The boys looked at each other then formed a huddle, including the ones on Jonathan's team. They discussed the matter in a whisper as Jonathan and Joanna waited. Then, nearly a minute later, they turned and faced the twins with mischievous grins on their faces and Darion stepped forward.

"I accept the Challenge," he said.

Jonathan grinned.

"But you can't phase shift," Darion added.

Jonathan shrugged. "I won't need to phase shift to beat you."

"First person to get knocked on their back loses," Darius announced. "Ready..."

Darion raised his fists to his face and Jonathan casually put his hands behind his back. Joanna and the rest of the boys backed away several steps to give Jonathan and Darion room.

"Set...fight!"

Darion waved his arms and the snow around him lifted into a giant white hammer. He swung his hand and the snow hammer flew at Jonathan's head. Jonathan kept his hands behind his back as he smoothly slid to the side and let the hammer swing past. Darion threw hammer after hammer at him, but each time, Jonathan dodged easily, as if the hammers were floating through an invisible sea of honey. This went on for about a minute longer with

Darion tossing various other snow weapons from swords, daggers, and even giant snow fists, and Jonathan casually dodging with his hands behind his back.

Then, as Darion was waving his hands to form the biggest snow hammer of the night, Jonathan flicked his fingers towards the stars and a pillar of snow shot up from beneath Darion's feet, tossing him into the air. Darion flipped several times before dropping to the ground. But before he could land on his back, Fred formed a pillow of snow that caught him and he slid off it gracefully then landed on his feet.

Then, as Jonathan was rolling his eyes at his own teammate helping out his opponent, the rest of the boys surrounded him and raised floating fists of snow aimed at him. He took a deep breath, knowing what was coming next, and shut his eyes as all the snow fists crashed into him at once, burying him beneath a frigid white mound.

"Sucker!" Darius shouted.

The rest of the boys snickered and hollered around the giant snow hill that had once been Jonathan.

"Boys rule!" they shouted as they ran away.

Joanna rushed over to the snow and blasted it with twin beams of fire until it melted into a mound of slush. Jonathan burst free, coughing and dripping wet from head to toe.

"Are you okay?" Joanna asked him, touching his face.

He knocked the side of his head and a few globs of slush popped out of his ear. "Should've seen that coming."

"You didn't have to do that," she told him.

"I didn't," he agreed. "But I wanted to. I'm not gonna let them leave you out like that."

Joanna smiled then kissed his cheek. "You're the best brother ever."

Jonathan lowered his head and sighed. Something was bothering him and his sister could tell that it was more than just how the boys had treated her.

"What's wrong?" she asked.

"I can't be the only boy who doesn't hate girls," he said. "It can't be that simple."

He looked at the igloos in the distance and spotted the boys high fiving each other and laughing.

"I think something's making the boys act like that," he said.

"Like, controlling them?" Joanna asked. "What could be doing that?"

Jonathan looked up at the moon and narrowed his eyes at it. "I don't know. But we're gonna find out."

"If something's controlling their minds," Joanna pondered. "You could always use your powers to find out."

Jonathan glared at her with a disapproving frown. "You've always said I'm not like other boys. I'm not gonna abuse my powers like that."

Joanna shrugged. "Just a suggestion."

Jonathan looked down at his palms and took a deep breath. "We'll figure it out. One way or another."

Chapter twenty-three

For the next year, Christina worked with white fire until she mastered it. In addition, Nana kept her promise of teaching Christina sign language. But whenever Christina would ask what purpose this played in her training, Nana would simply smile and say, "You'll find out one day."

Christina also learned that year that her fire could be released more powerfully with certain movements. As Nana said, "Flips fan flames." So as Christina learned to perform various acrobatic moves, she was able to release more fire with more power and in more shapes and sizes. Cartwheels released fire rings, back flips released fire bubbles, and back handsprings and back layouts released fire walls and fire sheets respectively. But above all, that year Nana began to teach Christina how to duel.

"Remember, your sword can cut through anything but metal," Nana was explaining.

They were standing in an open area where the ground was frozen white.

"Which means you'll have to learn to fight other swords," Nana went on.

"Who else has swords?" Christina asked. Her breath came out in puffs of cold air, but she still wasn't shivering as much as she had the first year.

"You'll find out when the time comes. First things first: defense." Without any further warning, she pulled a sword out from beneath her cloak and slashed the blade down towards Christina's head.

Christina shrieked and instinctively dropped the sword and ran away.

Nana chuckled. "This isn't the time to run away, child."

"Sorry," Christina said, walking back to her sword and picking it up. "Let me try again."

Nana slashed at her again and this time Christina held her ground and blocked the slash with her blade.

"Good," Nana congratulated her and held the position so both their swords remained locked. "But do you feel how unbalanced you are? Widen your feet and point your sword to the left..." Then she began to instruct Christina on the proper technique.

"Point your sword to the right," she would say. "Good. Point your sword at the ground...very good. Now hold your sword like you're scratching your back...good. Good."

They went on this way for an hour, Nana attacking and allowing Christina to instinctively defend then instructing her on the proper way until slowly but surely, Christina learned the technique of defending against various attacks.

As they dueled on, Christina moved much more fluidly, but Nana increased her attacks accordingly.

Christina blocked a strike from above then quickly pivoted to block a horizontal slash. Then she ducked and rolled as Nana swung at her head. She sprang to her feet and spun in time to block another slash. But the instant the two blades clashed, Nana unleashed a flurry of slashes upon Christina with such ferocity that it knocked the poor child to the ground.

"Get up," Nana told her.

Christina groaned and rubbed her arm as she climbed to her feet. "Could you go a little easy on me next time?"

Nana tilted her head at her curiously. "'Easy'? What does that mean?"

"You know. Just be a little—"

Nana banged her knuckles against Christina's forehead.

"Ow!" Christina cried. "What was *that* for?"

"You're a girl," Nana told her. "Nothing in life comes easy. Get used to it."

On they went dueling until Christina's arms were throbbing from not just from the cold, but from the battering of the blades.

***

When they retired to the cave that night, Christina was more than eager to eat dinner and go to sleep. But Nana had more things to teach her as they ate.

"I don't think I can take any more," Christina groaned as she drank her sea buckthorn tea.

"I'm sorry, I didn't know that I was asking for your permission," Nana told her. "You still have things to learn."

"Okay," Christina sighed, taking another bite of her grilled moose steak. Fuji nudged her arm with his nose and she rolled her eyes then dropped a piece for him.

"What is your mission?" Nana asked her.

"Melt the mountain, kill the serpent," Christina recited.

"What will happen when you melt the mountain?"

"The king will be freed and the kingdom will come."

"Very good," Nana added.

Christina furrowed her eyebrows as a thought occurred to her. "Nana, how do we know that King Christopher isn't..." She paused as she turned the question over in her mind, somewhat embarrassed to ask it. "I know that King Christopher is good and Emperor Andrew is bad...but how do we know that King Christopher's going to *stay* good? What if he makes things worse than Emperor Andrew?" Then another thought occurred to her. "Won't that be *my* fault? I'm replacing one boy with another boy."

Nana smirked. "Very clever, child. But you're mistaken. King Christopher is not a boy. He's much, much more than that. Boys can be selfish. The king is selfless. Boys can be mean. The king is kind. Boys can be crude. The king is pure."

Christina listened intently. She had only spoken with King Christopher once during her time in the tundra and still remembered the warmth she had felt from him. It had been quite a powerful encounter that she was sure she'd remember for the rest of her life. Nonetheless, it was still difficult to imagine a boy or a man who was as utterly good as Nana was describing. The only boy she had known who had ever been kind to her had been Jonathan.

"So you have no need to worry," Nana reassured her. "The king is good and he always will be. And besides, he won't be ruling alone."

"What do you mean?" Christina asked.

"As I told you before," Nana continued. "An empire grows through conquests. A kingdom grows through relationships. That's because an empire is ruled by a boy and a kingdom is ruled by a man and a woman--a king and a queen."

Christina's eyes widened in curiosity as she listened. "You mean they rule together? What's that like?"

"Oh, it's quite a sight to behold, child," Nana said, staring off absent-mindedly. It was as if she was remembering seeing the kingdom herself. "Boys need girls like the Earth needs the Sun. And girls need boys like the Earth needs the moon. When they work together, everything falls into their proper place."

"Wow," Christina said. "That...that sounds really beautiful." She lowered her moose steak without realizing it and Fuji grabbed it and devoured it.

"And you're going to teach the people that," Nana said, pointing at Christina's chest.

Christina smiled and felt a warmth growing inside her at the thought of it.

Chapter twenty-four

As Christina was spending her second year in the tundra training with white fire, the twins were spending that year focusing on their own endeavors. Jonathan and Joanna were now 15 years old. Joanna, like most girls her age, was supposed to be mastering the art of cooking without her powers since in 3 years she would no longer be able to create fire and would be expected to cook and clean with the best of the mothers. Jonathan, like most boys his age, was supposed to be in school learning to fight, train animals, and run businesses, or training to become a Crystal Lord. Neither of them were doing any of those things.

Joanna was more concerned with the mystical elements of fire and was failing miserably at cooking anything vaguely edible. Jonathan, on the other hand, had been obsessing over what could be controlling the boys and causing them to be so hostile towards girls. He'd observed the ones in his village during the day and at night to determine if their aggression levels changed at various times or during different phases of the moon. But he found the time of day or month had very little effect--they were equally hostile all year round. He even ventured to neighboring villages to see if the aggression varied by region. But it was the same across multiple villages in the Outer Ring--boys were simply aggressive to girls whenever and wherever he looked.

"You can always use your powers on them," Joanna repeatedly suggested.

"You can always stop saying that," he would always reply.

Instead, he targeted his powers in other means and studied the water, snow, and ice around him.

On this particular day, he was studying blocks of ice he had brought to the outskirts of the village.

He held a block floating in the air before him and shut his eyes as he allowed it to slowly twirl.

"Maybe different shapes affect our emotions," he said out loud to himself.

With a mere squeeze of his fingers, the cube flattened to a sheet. He tried to detect any change in his emotions, any hint of hostility or aggression, but felt nothing. He twisted his palm and the sheet twisted into a floating helix of ice. Still nothing.

"Tell me what you've seen," he said to the ice.

In an instant, a flash of white streaked across his mind's eye and he saw polar bears smashing through ice holes, penguins marching across snow, and fishermen chiseling chunks of ice out of glaciers.

He groaned. Reading ice was always unproductive. It didn't move much, so it was usually the same thing every time: animals and fishermen. But reading water was always messy because it was so fluid and would show him too much all at once: animals, girls, boys, food, urine, and poop, all swimming in a sea of emotions and memories of anyone who had stepped in, bathed in or drank it. He sighed. Maybe Joanna was right. But using this dimension of his powers on people felt so wrong. He felt that it should only be reserved for times of utmost necessity. Was this one of those times?

"Hungry?" Joanna said as she snuck up behind him.

Jonathan's eyes shot open and the ice helix dropped to the ground with a thud.

"No, actually," he said, making another block rise into the air.

"You find anything?" Joanna asked.

"Nothing much. And before you ask, the answer is still no."

"I wasn't gonna ask that."

"Yes you were."

"You're right."

"Have *you* found anything interesting?"

"Actually, I have," Joanna said, a note of excitement in her voice. "I've been watching Christina through my fire."

Jonathan raised an eyebrow and nodded his approval. "That's so cool that you can do that. Is this how you feel watching me all the time?"

"If you mean confused, bored, and close to vomiting from the smell of your farts, then yes. That's exactly how I feel."

"My farts smell like well-seasoned seal meat, thank you very much. I can't say the same about yours."

"Anyway," Joanna continued. "She's being trained by an old woman. I don't know where she came from. I've never seen her before, but her fire is extremely powerful. I can feel her even when I'm not looking for her."

"Hmmm," Jonathan said. "Glad our cousin's in good company."

"On another note," Joanna stepped around and stood in front of him. "Will you try this for me?"

Jonathan looked down at the wooden plate in her hands. On top was a white slab of meat with black and green specs on it. Jonathan wasn't sure what it was supposed to be and, quite frankly, neither am I. I haven't the vaguest idea what the child had attempted to cook this time.

"I'm not sure if you knew this," Jonathan began. "But when I said I wasn't hungry, that meant...I wasn't hungry."

"Please, Jonathan," she begged him. "I've gotten better, I promise!"

"That's what you said last time."

"But it's true!"

"Look, you don't have to be good at cooking just because you're a girl."

"And you don't have to protect me just because you're a boy."

Jonathan lifted his finger to raise a counter argument then dropped his hand in defeat. "Well played." He took a deep breath then grabbed the slab of meat. He lifted it to his mouth as his sister watched in anticipation, took a delicate bite, then chewed.

She waited eagerly for him to swallow and when he did, he immediately bent over and spit into the snow.

"So...?" she said.

"Great...," he breathed, gagging on his hands and knees. "It tastes a lot less like poop."

Joanna laughed. "I told you I got better."

Chapter twenty-five

It took Christina a few more days of practice to finally get the hang of the basics of sword fighting. But one afternoon, Nana gave her a break from the swordplay and sent her on a task to "tag a rabbit".

Christina hid behind a boulder and eyed the furry creature nearly a hundred yards away, nibbling on something Christina couldn't see. Her task was simple: land one single flame on the rabbit's tail. It would naturally scurry away and bury its tail into the snow to put the fire out and Christina would have accomplished her task. But if Christina missed, the rabbit would hop away much too quickly for her to catch again. This was both an exercise in stealth and accuracy. For in order to land a proper hit, she had to be close.

A bow and arrow would've been nice, Nana, she thought to herself. *But no. Let's make things as hard as possible for Christina. Let's push Christina to her limits.* She scoffed to herself. *I can do this.*

Naturally, Fuji had wanted to tag along for the hunt. Naturally, Christina had declined. Yet now a small part of her wondered if he would have been helpful at sniffing this rabbit out if it happened to run away before she could tag it. She shook the thoughts out of her head and slowly crept out from behind the boulder. The rabbit remained with its back to her and continued nibbling on its snack. She hurried behind another boulder closer to it and its ears perked up.

Don't move. Don't move. It's nothing.

As if it could hear her thoughts, it sprang forward and leapt deeper into the fog of the tundra.

Blazes! Christina rushed out from behind the boulder and hurried after the rabbit. There weren't any trees or bushes for it to hide behind or holes in the ground for it to disappear into so for the moment she had a slight advantage. But it was much quicker than she was and steadily widened the gap between them as it hopped away.

"Get back here!" she shouted, firing a blast of flames at it. It hopped to the right and the flames narrowly missed it.

The rabbit led her on for several hundred yards, up hills and down valleys, across frozen streams and through caves. She was both grateful and confused that the rabbit hadn't found a good hiding place by now. Had it wandered that far from home? Or was it teasing her? Soon the fog gave way to dead shrubs and the frozen ground was replaced by soft snow. The silence of the tundra was replaced by distant sounds Christina had almost forgotten existed. She stopped and craned her head to listen better. Voices. There were voices nearby!

The rabbit finally disappeared in a hole near an igloo, but Christina ignored it. She had left the tundra and had entered the edge of her home village.

Stay focused, she could almost hear Nana tell her.

But her curiosity got the best of her and she jogged further into the edge of the village, searching for the voices.

"Leave me alone!" she heard someone shout.

It was a little girl.

"Where you goin'?" A boy.

"She looks dirty," another boy said. "She needs a bath. Let's give her one!"

There was boisterous laughing from other boys and the girl shrieked. They were Crystal Lords and they were bullying an innocent little girl.

Christina followed the voices until she came upon several igloos where the boys were surrounding a little girl in a gray parka. There were three of them and two were holding the girl while the third was spraying ice cold water into her face. Christina felt her fire rising inside at the sight and made her hands into fists. She couldn't let this happen. Not on her watch. But she paused momentarily. There were three boys and only one Christina. What if they overpowered her? Then she remembered the pouch of salt in her pocket Jonathan had given her. If push came to shove, she could simply throw salt onto them and they couldn't freeze her. With that settled she jumped into the open and interrupted the bullying.

"Hey!" she shouted. "Back off!"

The boys stopped and turned to her.

"Who are you?" the one who had been spraying asked. He stood several heads taller than Christina and the other boys and she assumed he was the leader.

Christina pulled her sword out and pointed it at the boys. "Your worst nightmare."

The boys glanced at each other and laughed. Then they roared and charged Christina, sending blasts of water and ice her way. This may be the part where you're expecting Christina to deal these bullies a handsome beating. Unfortunately, this is not what happened. Instead, it was the boys who gave Christina the beating.

She tried to fight them off with her sword, but they simply kept their distance and knocked her in the head with frozen snowballs.

Then they sprayed her with streams of bitter cold water, shutting down her powers and further humiliating her. She fell onto her backside, spitting up water into the snow, and crab-walked away as the boys marched towards her. Then she reached into her pocket for the pouch of salt. Push had certainly come to shove and this would be her saving grace.

She yanked the pouch out, but before she could reach over with her other hand to grab the salt inside, one of the Crystal Lords shot her hand, freezing it to the pouch in a block of ice.

Christina yelped in pain, but continued crab-walking away. The boys picked up the pace and started running towards her. She had to get away. Soon, they would be upon her and there was no telling what they would do to her. She scrambled to her feet and sprinted through the village back the way she had come. The boys sent flurries of icicles after her, slashing up her neck and legs and forcing her to stumble the whole way. Finally, she made it back into the tundra and heard the boys stop behind her.

"Don't you ever come back!" they shouted. "Stupid girl!"

Christina ran on for a few more meters before dropping to her hands and knees, wheezing and out of breath.

Then, in the midst of her desperate attempt to catch her breath, a pair of boots entered her vision and she looked up to see Nana standing over her. Christina had expected to be greeted with concern, but the frown on Nana's face dashed that expectation as she asked Christina one question: "What did I tell you?"

Chapter twenty-six

"I was tagging the rabbit," Christina stammered. "But it ran away...and I....I ran back into the village...and there were these boys attacking a girl..." She spit on the ground and blood stained the snow. Then something occurred to her. "You were here the whole time?"

Nana stared back at her with that same stern look carved into her face.

"Why didn't you help me?" Christina asked her, shakily climbing to her feet.

"You were supposed to tag a rabbit," Nana replied. "Not get into fights you have no business getting yourself into."

"That girl needed help so I tried to help her," Christina explained. She winced from the cold of her frozen hand still encased in ice. "I thought I was strong enough..." She lowered her head then looked back up quickly. "But why didn't you just step in?"

"I'm not always going to be there to protect you. This will remind you that perfection is not an option. It's the only way to survive. Your footing was off, you were telegraphing your moves, you--"

"Are you kidding me?!" Christina cried, throwing her hands in the air. "I could've died!"

"Because of your mistakes, Christina!"

Christina fell silent and stared at the snow, her wrist numb from her frozen hand. Nana stepped up to her, grabbed the ice in her hand, and released a steady flow of white fire into it. Within moments, the ice was melting and Christina was able to shake her hand free.

Nana gave her no time to celebrate or even thank her. She looked Christina straight in her eyes and told her, "The sooner you learn that perfection is the only way to survive the better."

Christina lowered her head and followed Nana back to the cave without another word.

*****

While Christina was being scolded by Nana, Joanna was being scolded by her own mother while attempting to cook salmon. She had successfully caught the salmon, but was unsuccessfully seasoning it. They were a short distance away from the village and had already skinned the salmon. It was now sitting in a clay pan over a fire Joanna had started without using her powers.

"That's far too much salt!" Mother scolded her, pulling Joanna's hand away from the pan. "It was supposed to be a sprinkle, Joanna."

"Sorry," Joanna shrugged.

Suddenly, she heard commotion back at the village and her and Mother craned their heads to see what was happening. As they did, they spotted several Crystal Lords skating on ice tracks through the air into the village.

"They're here!" Mother gasped. "Joanna, hurry!"

Joanna extinguished the fire under the pan with a wave of her hand then joined Mother in sprinting back to the igloo. Mother rushed inside as Joanna and Father stood side by side at the entrance, watching the Crystal Lords stroll triumphantly in front of the villagers.

There were five of them and one, the tallest by far of the group, was making it very clear that he was the leader.

"You know what time it is, poor, dirty, Outer Ringers!" he shouted. "Tax time! And I, Lord Dangerous, am here to collect it."

"Lord Dangerous?" Joanna whispered to Father. "I didn't even know that was a real title."

"It's not," Father whispered back. "He's trying to make himself sound important."

"Lord Dangerous" stopped at an igloo and snatched the pouch of money from the parents at the entrance. He went from igloo to igloo, reminding them of his made-up title and making new, disparaging remarks about the village with each igloo he visited.

"This village stinks like a seal's butt cheeks," he said to one.

"You all look like you're poor," he said to another. "Oh, I forgot. You *are!*"

"Mother, hurry!" Joanna whispered into the igloo. "They're coming!"

But Mother was still rummaging inside. Joanna stood as straight as she could next to Father as Lord Dangerous and his group approached the igloo. They were laughing at the mean joke he had just said about the prior family when they finally stopped and stared at Joanna and Father.

"Pay up," Lord Dangerous said.

"We will," Father replied. "Just one moment."

"Do I look like I have moments?" Lord Dangerous snapped. "You pay up now or--"

"My lords!" Mother rushed out of the igloo, waving a small leather pouch in her hand, and nearly ran straight into the Crystal Lords. "I'm sorry for the delay."

Lord Dangerous snatched the pouch from her and peered inside. Then he handed the pouch to one of the Crystal Lords on his left and crossed his hands in front of his waist.

"You made me wait," he announced. "That'll be five more gold coins."

"What?" Father asked. "We don't have any more. Those were our last coins. We paid you what we owe."

"What you owe me, is respect, old man!" Lord Dangerous shouted. "Didn't you hear my name? I am dangerous!"

"Yeah!" another Crystal Lord shouted. "Dangerous! Like fire!"

"No!" Lord Dangerous scolded him. "Not like fire! I'm not a girl."

"Sorry," the Crystal Lord apologized.

"Anyway," Lord Dangerous continued. "You need to pay a late fee or I'm gonna have to figure out some way to make you pay. Is that what you want?"

"We don't want any trouble," Joanna chimed in. "We just don't have the money right--"

"I'm sorry, sweetie, was I talking to you?" Lord Dangerous snapped. "Didn't your parents teach you not to talk when boys are talking?"

"I'm sorry," Joanna lowered her head.

"You really are," Lord Dangerous said. "That's another five gold coins."

"What?!" Father and Mother cried.

"Please," Father pleaded. "We can't afford that."

"You should've thought about that," Lord Dangerous shrugged. "Before you disrespected me. Now pay up before--"

"I knew it smelled like rats out here," Jonathan laughed as he marched onto the scene. "For guys who can control water, you'd think you'd shower once in a while."

"You watch your mouth, boy," Lord Dangerous growled. "I'm dangerous."

"Hi, Dangerous," Jonathan held his hand out. "I'm Not Impressed. Nice to meet you. Listen, you heard my family, we don't have any more money. We're sorry we hurt your feelings, but we don't have anything else to give."

"Pay up, or it's gonna get really ugly really fast."

Jonathan pinched the bridge of his nose and sighed. "I'm gonna start over. Tell me where I lose you. We. Have. No. Money. You took all of it."

"Well," Lord Dangerous snickered. "If you can't pay, then we'll just take your sister."

Mother and Father gasped.

"Emperor Andrew is always looking for new servant girls," Lord Dangerous added.

Jonathan's hands instantly curled into firsts at his sides.

"Don't touch her," he warned.

"Don't touch who?" Lord Dangerous asked, stepping closer to Joanna.

"Please," Father said. "Leave my--"

"Shut up, old man!" Lord Dangerous ordered and all the Crystal Lords aimed spears of ice at him to keep him back.

Joanna swallowed nervously as Lord Dangerous approached her and looked her up and down. He reached up to her head and pulled her hood off, letting her dreadlocks fall to her shoulders.

Jonathan's breath came out in angry hisses. "I'm warning you."

"You look like you'd be a really great servant," Lord Dangerous said. "If you won't give me respect, maybe I should just take it." In an instant, he grabbed her face and leaned in to kiss her. But before his lips could touch hers, Jonathan had snatched his wrist away, spun him around into a headlock, then slammed him to the ground on his knees. Jonathan pressed his fingers against Lord Dangerous' forehead and immediately, like water bursting from a dam into a river, Lord Dangerous' memories and desires burst into Jonathan's fingers and into his own mind.

The Crystal Lords rushed forward, aiming their ice spears at him, but he had already seen everything he'd needed to see.

"Stay back!" Jonathan ordered them. "Or I'll snap little Dinah's neck."

The Crystal Lords murmured to each other.

"How?" Lord Dangerous stammered. "How do you know my name?"

"Dinah?" the Crystal Lords asked one another. "Isn't that a girl's name?"

"Dinah of the Outer Ring," Jonathan went on, squeezing the Crystal Lord's neck tighter. "Isn't that right, 'Lord Dangerous'?"

Dinah gasped in shock and his eyes darted back and forth to the Crystal Lords watching in equal shock.

"Now leave," Jonathan warned. "Before I tell your friends what you do with crab legs on your free time." He pushed Dinah forward and he quickly scrambled to his feet. Within moments, the Crystal Lords were hopping on ice tracks and skating away.

The villagers cheered to see them leave, but Jonathan was already marching away from the igloo, Joanna rushing to keep up with him.

"You used your powers on him!" she said, gleefully. "Did you see it? Did you find out what's controlling them?"

Jonathan kept marching without even glancing at her. There was a look of concern engraved on his face and Joanna did not like it one bit.

"No," he finally said.

They stopped when they were out of earshot of the village.

Joanna was confused. "Then why do you look so worried? And why did you come all the way over here to tell me that?" She studied his face as he stared down at the snow. "What *did* you see?"

"The Emperor is planning something," he said slowly. "And the Crystal Lords are excited about it."

"Planning? The Emperor?" Joanna scoffed. "He's dumber than a trout. What can he possibly be planning?"

"I don't know," Jonathan said. "And neither do the Crystal Lords. They just know something's coming." He took a deep breath then turned to his sister. "But if it's good news for boys, then it's bad news for girls."

Chapter twenty-seven

Christina didn't speak to Nana for the rest of the day. She was both ashamed for having disappointed her, but also upset that Nana hadn't helped her.

When night arrived and they had both retired to the cave, Christina sat in front of the fire and stared at the flames in utter silence, rehearsing everything she had done wrong that day. Fuji sensed that she was upset and lay near her feet, but she paid him no mind.

If she hadn't been so slow, she would've caught the rabbit. If she had isolated the boys instead of taking them on all at once, she could have beaten them. She should have recruited the girl to help her so that she wouldn't have been so outnumbered. She should have used the salt on the boys from the beginning to give herself an early advantage.

Nana stepped in front of her, holding a cup of tea. At first Christina didn't even lift her head. She was still focusing on how she could correct her mistakes.

"I'm hard on you because I care," Nana told her. Then she breathed a heavy sigh. "And I push you because I know what you're capable of."

She held the cup out and Christina took a deep breath before taking it from her.

"Thank you," Christina said.

As she drank, she felt a warmth in her heart from both the tea and from Nana's words.

***

After that brutal beating by the Crystal Lords, Christina was determined to never let herself be defeated again. From then on, she spent every free moment she had practicing whatever Nana had taught her that day. Several weeks later, on this particular night, she was practicing parries.

"Point to the left...point to the right...point at the ground...scratch your back..." she whispered to herself as she moved across the snow. The glow of the sword danced across the surface of boulders around her in the dark. "Point to the left...point to the right...scratch your back...point to the...No. C'mon, Christina!"

She walked in circles a few times to reorient herself then tried again. "Point to the left...point to the right..." She performed the sequence until her footprints had formed deep ruts criss crossing in the snow.

She had been spending her mornings and afternoons practicing her techniques, trying to cement the movements into her mind and body. But it was more than simply practice that brought her outside tonight.

"Point to the left...point to the right..." A memory of Dom smacking her back with ice cold water streaked through her mind and she hissed to control herself. "Point at the ground...scratch your back..." A memory of Dom pouring a stream of water on her face to wake her up streaked through next and she threw her sword to the ground, screaming.

"Trouble sleeping?"

Christina spun to see Nana standing in the snow behind her.

"I..." she started. "Uh...yeah."

"What's on your mind?"

Christina sat down with her arms over her knees. "It's Dom. I keep remembering all the stuff he's done to me. And I'm getting bitter again. I thought I forgave him. Why do I still feel so bitter?"

Nana took several steps towards her and stopped in front of her. "Bitterness is like ice. It takes time to melt it."

"Well, what do I do?"

Nana tapped Christina's legs with her foot and Christina shifted so she was sitting cross legged. "Close your eyes...open your hands...now simmer."

Christina followed the instructions, but sighed as she did. She wasn't really interested in doing this.

"Let the memories come," Nana told her.

Christina sighed again. That part would be easy. As she sat there, the memories came pouring in. Dom smacking her back. Dom pouring water on her while she slept. Dom scratching the back of her legs with icicles. Dom letting dogs loose to chase her through the village.

Finally she stopped and shook her head. "What is this gonna do? I remember what he did. That's not the problem."

"Who's giving the instructions here?"

"Sorry."

"And close your eyes."

"Sorry."

"White fire is blocked by bitterness and released by forgiveness. So you when you simmer, you can deal with the bitterness that's still inside you."

"But I thought I already forgave him," Christina said. "I have to forgive him again? How many times?"

"How many times did he hurt you?"

"I don't even know."

"Exactly. Now simmer."

Christina sighed and formed a ball of orange fire in her palms. She let the memories return little by little and the anger and bitterness rose inside of her as they came. The smacking. The pouring. The scratching. The chasing. With each memory, she felt her blood heating up and her heart racing until she wanted to jump up and scream.

But she didn't.

Instead, she sat still and let her orange fire burn.

"Forgive him," she heard Nana say. "Again."

She focused on the memories one by one. Dom smacking her in the back.

I should've smacked you in the back, she thought to herself. But she took a deep breath and remembered what Nana had been teaching her. Boys weren't the enemy.

"I forgive you," she said out loud. "For smacking me in the back with that water."

After the words were out, she felt something cold inside of her give way to a new warmth.

One by one she went through each memory and forgave Dom for each one until her chest was baking with the new warmth. When she opened her eyes, her orange ball of fire had turned completely white.

"Forgiveness takes time," Nana said above her. "But whenever you feel the bitterness come back, let the forgiveness simmer."

Christina nodded and a tear dropped down her cheek and into the fire with a sizzle.

Chapter twenty-eight

On the other side of the empire, quite a different turn of events was transpiring. Jonathan and Joanna were on a hunt. Their food was running out and if they didn't find some game, the village would be forced to relocate somewhere else in the empire. This was all quite normal, but also quite tiresome. If Jonathan and Joanna could find a large enough animal like a polar bear, for example, it could feed the entire village and they wouldn't have to move.

Normally, men and boys would go on hunts and the girls and women would cook what they killed. But on this particular night, it just so happened that another lunar eclipse was occuring. If you've been keeping track of them, you may now know that lunar eclipses occur about twice every three years. Because of this, all the boys and men in all the villages in Andromeno were performing their own local Rain Ceremonies to remind the girls and women who were in charge. Jonathan had opted out of participating, as he usually did, and instead decided to go hunting with his sister.

The twins walked through a patch of evergreen trees to a dark figure in a clearing up ahead. When they were within about a hundred meters, Jonathan held his fist up for Joanna to stop and they both paused at the edge of the clearing.

The figure was an elk, tall and bulky, with thick antlers reaching for the sky. It was staring straight above, as if it were in awe of the Earth's shadow creeping across the moon as the eclipse began.

Jonathan nodded to Joanna. "You know the drill."

Joanna went on the move and slowly made her way around to the front of the elk. When she was about fifty meters in front of it, it snorted and stared at her.

"Hey, Mr. Elk," she said, soothingly. "Everything's gonna be alright."

It snorted as it looked her up and down, apparently deciding whether or not she was a threat. Little did it know that while Joanna was distracting her in the front, Jonathan was sneaking up from behind it. Then, before it even knew what had happened, it was frozen from head to toe in a thick coat of ice.

Jonathan walked out from behind it, wiping his hands triumphantly.

"Great job, as usual, sis," he congratulated her.

She bowed dramatically. "Thank you. I couldn't have done it without you."

"Awww, you're too kind," Jonathan said. "But please...go on."

Joanna chucked then walked up to the elk. "This is perfect. It will be enough to feed the entire village. Mother and Father will be so happy."

"Yeah," Jonathan agreed. Then he scratched his chin. "But how are we gonna carry it?"

They paced around the frozen beast for a few moments, trying to figure out how they would transport it back to the village. They couldn't leave it here to get help from the villagers or they'd risk other hunters stealing it while they were gone. Then, when they were wondering which one of them should stay, an arrow suddenly stabbed the snow at Jonathan's feet.

He glanced down at it for a second and was grateful it had missed his toes by a few inches.

By the time he looked back up, a group of girls in black parkas and fiery red masks came flipping through the air and landed in a circle around him, Joanna, and the elk.

"Rebels," he nodded. "Of course."

"Hand over the elk," one of them said, aiming her bow at Jonathan.

Jonathan held his hands up in surrender and glanced around at the group. There were about seven of them total and they had all surrounded them in a complete circle by now, blocking any way of escape.

"Funny you should say that," he said. "It's a little too heavy to hand over sooooo...we're gonna have to say no to that. Come back next time."

The Rebel leader shot another arrow and this one hit even closer to Jonathan's toes.

"I'm not gonna say it again," she said.

Joanna touched Jonathan's shoulder as she stepped up. "Let me talk to them."

She took a few steps forward and kept her hands in the air to show that she wasn't intending to fight. "We're trying to feed our village. We've run out of food and might have to migrate. But if you guys need food too, why don't we split the elk?"

The Rebel leader cocked her head to the side curiously, as if she were thinking it over.

"Sharing isn't our strong suit," she replied. "But you look like a smart girl. Why don't you join us?"

Joanna smiled politely. "I'm flattered, but no thank you. I'd rather stay with my family. My brother and I really need to be on our way."

"Is that so?" the Rebel leader scoffed. "Your loyalty is misplaced. One day, your brother will turn on you. They all do."

Joanna shook her head. "Jonathan is different. He's not like other boys. Trust me, I--"

"Enough!" The Rebel pulled her bowstring back further. "You either give us the elk or we take it from you."

"We don't want any trouble," Joanna said. "Can we not fight?"

"Yeah," Jonathan agreed. "I don't fight girls."

"Well good news," the Rebel leader said, aiming her bow at him now. "We're not girls. We're Rebels."

She fired an arrow and Jonathan barely managed to erect a block of ice to deflect it. He and Joanna rushed underneath the frozen elk, but some arrows pierced their feet and ankles. They couldn't hide behind it either because they would be exposed to the Rebels on that side.

"We have to fight," Jonathan told Joanna.

"I'd rather not," Joanna replied.

An arrow flew past her, ripping a piece of her sleeve as it did.

"And I'd rather not die," Jonathan said. He jumped out into the open and raised his arms above him. Immediately, a wave of snow rose from the ground, curled over the Rebels in front of him in a powdery tsunami, and crashed on top of them.

"I don't wanna hurt you," he explained.

They paid him no mind. Even though they were now wet and powerless, they charged him fearlessly and sent arrows flying his way as they did.

He ran away, arrows piercing the snow in jagged lines behind him.

"Eclipse, if you could hurry it up, that'd be great!" he shouted at the sky.

Meanwhile, Joanna forced herself out of hiding and launched fireball after fireball at the Rebels on her end. They all easily evaded her attacks and charged her with onslaughts of arrows as well until she was backing into the frozen elk again.

Within a few minutes, the Rebels had Jonathan tied by his hands and feet and had Joanna tied to a tree, dripping in snow. With the twins out of the way, the Rebels proceeded to melt the ice, cut the elk into pieces, then carried the pieces away.

"Thanks for dinner," the leader said as she marched past Joanna.

Joanna watched them disappear deeper into the trees just as the Earth's shadow completely veiled the moon.

"Well, that was embarrassing," Jonathan sighed.

"What are we gonna do now?" Joanna asked. "We don't have any more food."

Jonathan maneuvered his fingers behind his back and within a few seconds had fashioned some snow into an ice dagger. He used it to cut off the ropes around his wrists then cut his ankles free. Then he jogged over to Joanna and cut her free as well.

"C'mon," he said. "We can start hunting for-- whoa!" His eyes suddenly flashed with blue light and he jumped back as if he had been struck by a bolt of lightning. Joanna looked up at the sky and saw the blood red moon hanging above them. The eclipse had begun.

Jonathan groaned as he threw his hands to his head, as if he were afraid something was about to burst from the inside of it.

"Are you okay?" Joanna asked him. She was used to seeing him overwhelmed with the moon's power during an eclipse, but it was never painful. Something wasn't quite right. "What's happening?"

"I don't know," Jonathan breathed, staggering forward. "There's so much...so much..." He couldn't find the words to explain what was happening. See, since Jonathan was a peculiar boy, being that he had the special ability to "read" water, lunar eclipses affected him differently. His powers were already much more elevated than regular boys so during eclipses his powers would skyrocket to nearly unbearable levels. But they were rarely ever painful. Tonight, however, it *was* painful. For he was able to hear the thoughts of every boy and man in the empire. With thousands of thoughts flooding his mind, he was sure that his head was about to explode.

He dropped on his hands and knees and the instant his palms touched the snow, his mind was washed with memories. He saw children eating, mothers cooking, fathers laughing, boys chasing girls, salmon swimming upstream, polar bears attacking hunters, and falcons being shot down with arrows. But there was something underneath it all, a quiet hum that whispered a secret into his mind he had not anticipated.

Joanna stood over her brother, unsure whether she should touch him or leave him alone. She had never seen him react this way to an eclipse before and had no idea what to do. So she simply watched, holding her hand to her mouth and hoping he would be okay.

Finally, several minutes later, Jonathan stood to his feet, breathing heavily. The moon was still red and his eyes were still blue, but he seemed much more stable now.

"What did you see?" Joanna asked him.

He took several heavy breaths before slowly turning to her.

"It's the serpent," he told her. "He's using something to control boys."

Joanna's jaw dropped. "The serpent? From the legend? What is he using?"

Jonathan shook his head. "I don't know. But we have to find out soon."

Chapter twenty-nine

For the next year, Christina trained relentlessly with her white fire. Just as she had done with her swordplay, she spent every free moment she had perfecting her fire: forming fireballs, creating campfires, simmering, and even cooking for Nana and Fuji. Eventually, she mastered white fire as much as she had mastered orange fire and it was time to move on to the next level.

One day Nana brought Christina to a giant sheet of ice and walked her across it. Christina wondered what they were going to do. Was it another fight? Was there something else that she would discover fire could do? But soon Nana stopped at a large hole in the ice and Christina realized with a shock what this was. This wasn't a sheet of ice. This was a frozen lake and this hole was an ice hole. Immediately, she froze in her spot and stared at Nana.

"What is this?" she asked, her voice shaking.

"This is an ice hole, Christina. I'm sure you've seen one of them before."

"Is this a joke? Are you punishing me?"

"No. Do you want to be punished?"

"No."

"Then stop talking and listen. The last level of fire is blue fire. It's the hottest of all fires. It's blocked by fear and is released by love."

Christina looked at the ice hole then back at Nana. "So you're making me face my fear. By trying to drown me?"

"There are methods to my madness. You know this."

"I don't get it. How is love supposed to help me overcome my fear? Shouldn't it be courage?"

"Shouldn't you not be asking stupid questions?"

"Stupid is better than crazy!" Christina countered. "You're trying to drown me! I don't need love. I need courage. Can blue fire give me some of that?"

Nana sighed deeply and shook her head. "Love drives out fear. Because when you love someone, no fear can ever stop you from protecting them."

Christina thought about that for a moment then looked back at the ice hole. By the time she looked back up, Nana was holding a rope in her hands. Before Christina could protest, Nana had tied the rope around Christina's waist.

"Wait," said Christina. "What are you doing?"

"You're going into the water," Nana said. "If you get too afraid, tug the rope and I'll pull you out."

"Wait! Can I get some time to get ready first?"

"Fear doesn't wait for you to get ready," Nana told her. With that she pushed Christina into the hole.

Christina's body dropped for several seconds through emptiness without touching any water. At first she was confused but then she remembered that this was the tundra so there were probably dozens of feet of ice before the water. She wondered how Nana had managed to melt a hole so deep through the ice and was quite impressed by this. Just as she was thinking this, her body hit the water and burst with an explosion of cold on every inch of her.

She sank deeper and deeper into the water and kicked her feet and waved her arms, but it was no use. She couldn't swim. Eventually her body floated somewhere far above the bottom of the lake. But even though she was now still, it didn't mean she was calm. She was still terrifyingly cold.

Then, just when she thought things couldn't get any scarier, her worst fear materialized. A dark shadow slowly ascended through the water towards her as if the trunk of a massive oak tree was floating up from the deep beneath her. At first Christina didn't even realize that it was a creature when it neared for all of the water around her grew ominously dark. It appeared as if the lake had suddenly become tainted with a black liquid. But soon Christina realized this was not a liquid at all. It most certainly was not the trunk of a tree, either. This was a creature so large its body was blocking out the little light that was still visible underwater. It swam in a slow deliberate circle, surrounding her in darkness thicker than the water she was in.

Chrissssstina.

The Sea Serpent turned its head towards her, piercing her with the gaze of its glowing green slits for eyes. Then it opened its jaws and revealed its long white fangs. Christina panicked and quickly yanked on the rope as hard and as many times as she could. The Sea Serpent opened its jaws again and swam closer to her. But before it could reach her Nana pulled Christina up out of the water, up through the hole, and onto the surface of the ice.

Christina gasped for air and shivered uncontrollably from head to toe. There was a coal fire burning on the ice and Nana threw a warm blanket over Christina.

"You gave in to your fear," Nana said.

Christina wanted to scream something at her—something very mean and impolite of course—but her jaws were shaking too much for her to form any words. Besides, she was still too cold to even think straight. All she could see was the serpent's fangs in her mind. All she could hear was its voice hissing her name. All she could feel was the bitter cold fear gripping her body and her heart.

"Love drives out fear," Nana said. "When fear comes again, think of the ones you love. And remember that they're counting on you to overcome this fear."

Christina just sat there shivering. But little by little as her body got warmer she began to take in Nana's words. She remembered Cindy. And Mother. And Father. And Caroline. She remembered how much she loved them and how much they loved her. But they were all gone. Did that still count? Could this still work?

She took a deep breath then took the blanket off and stood to her feet.

"Ready?" Nana asked.

Christina nodded and before the nod was even done the old woman pushed her back into the hole. Christina splashed through the water, felt the shock of the cold again, and floated above the bottom of the lake again. Just as before, the Sea Serpent came again and encircled her. But this time Christina didn't panic. She stayed floating and watched it stare at her.

Chrissssstina.

Christina stared back.

Chosssen One.

Christina's heart was racing. Hearing the serpent's voice in her mind was somehow more terrifying than seeing it before her. It felt so exposing, so invasive, as if there was nowhere she could hide from it. She wanted to escape and never return, but she forced herself to resist the urge to yank the rope.

If you really are the Chosssen One, the serpent taunted her. *Fight me.*

Christina stared back at it. Her heart was still racing and at this point she was running out of breath and on the verge of panic. Fight it? She couldn't do that. It would eat her alive.

Then the serpent opened its jaws again and lunged at her again. Christina tried to think of her family. Of how much she loved them. Of how much they meant to her. But in this moment, her fear overtook her again and she yanked the rope again. Again Nana pulled her out of the hole and onto the surface and wrapped the blanket around her.

When Christina was warm enough to speak, she kept her eyes on the ice and said, "I'm too scared."

Nana gently rubbed her shoulders as she sighed.

"Isn't t-t-t-there another way?" Christina asked, still shivering. "Can't I just use the s-s-s-sword? Why do I have to release this fire, anyway? I already have t-t-t-the other three. Isn't that enough?"

Nana turned Christina so that she was facing her. "All of the fires you've learned to make can be put out by water. But there are some fires that even water can't put out. This is one of them."

Christina shook her head. "But I can't d-d-d-do it."

"You can," Nana said. "And one day you will."

"Can't I just melt the mountain without having to fight the Serpent?"

Nana sighed and rubbed Christina's shoulder. "If only it were that easy."

For Nana knew something Christina did not. That while they were talking above the ice hole the Sea Serpent had already swam far from them beneath the ice hole. For the water under the tundra was connected to the rivers that ran through the villages, which were connected to the Crystal Lake, which was connected to pools inside the Crystal Mountain. At that very moment, even, the Sea Serpent was already swimming inside the mountain, plotting and preparing for its inevitable encounter. So you see no matter where Christina went in the empire, she could never run from the Serpent. If she didn't master blue fire, the Serpent would eventually master her.

Chapter thirty

Christina continued to train with Nana at the ice hole every night, desperate to master blue fire. But every night, she would fail time and time again. Many times the serpent wasn't even present and Christina would panic from the mere thought of it suddenly appearing. Each time, Nana would encourage her that one day she would master blue fire. But Christina began to doubt that she ever would.

On one particular night, Nana and Christina were heading back to the cave for dinner. It seemed like another ordinary night, like every other ordinary night that had come before it. But many a terrible thing have happened on seemingly ordinary nights. Little did they know that tonight would be such a night.

"It's your turn to cook dinner," Nana informed Christina.

"Really?" Christina whined. "But I cooked last--"

Suddenly, a roar drowned out her voice and stopped her in her tracks.

"What was that?" she asked, drawing her sword.

Nana looked to the left as a second roar came, this one from another direction.

Christina whirled, aiming her sword at wherever these roars were coming from.

"Are those what I think they are?" she asked, trying to keep her voice from trembling.

"Yes," Nana said. "Crystal Beasts. Christina, stay close. We have to fight."

A third roar came. Then a fourth. Then a fifth. Then several others. Christina shook her head and put her sword back in her scabbard.

"No, Nana," she replied. "There's too many of them. We have to run!"

"Stop being a baby," Nana reprimanded her. "Haven't I taught you to fight?"

"I beat one Crystal Beast. Not seven! I'm not ready."

"Well, I suggest you change that immediately," Nana said.

With that, three Crystal Beasts stomped into view in front of her, towering over her like misshapen frozen trees. Three more appeared in front of Christina and she backpedaled until she bumped into Nana's back. Fuji snarled at them at her side, ready to pounce.

The beasts roared and the sound made Christina's knees buckle. Before she even had a chance to remove her sword again, they charged and the ground shook with their stomps.

Nana released streams of white fire as they came and they cried in pain from the flames, but continued crashing forward, their arms sizzling from where the fire had hit them. Christina ran around, ducking and rolling underneath the swings of their massive, frozen fists, while Fuji attempted to take bites out of their feet. She dove into front flips, cartwheels, and back handsprings, releasing fires in all shapes and sizes with every flip that Nana had taught her.

The three of them fought the beasts off with all the fire and biting they could muster. Nana eventually managed to melt one of them and the resulting boy scrambled away. Christina was even able to turn one as well. But there were still five beasts left and with all of them ganging up on them at once, it was remarkably difficult to focus their fire on just one at a time.

"We have to go!" Christina cried, swinging her sword at a beast's leg as it came at her. She slashed its thigh and it sizzled slightly, but the sword barely cut through its ice. "There's too many of them!"

Then, as if to confirm her fears, a Crystal Beast marched up from behind Nana and struck her with a vicious backhanded smack, sending her flying through the air and landing several feet away.

"Nana!" Christina shrieked, running towards her. But before she had even taken two steps, another beast backhanded her into the opposite direction. Christina hit the ground face first and rolled wildly until she finally flopped onto her back. Her ears were ringing, her head was spinning, and she was seeing double as she tried to sit up. Then, to seal her fate, one of the beasts shot a blast of ice at her that froze her legs to the ground.

Christina gasped in panic and felt around for her sword, but her fingers touched nothing but cold hard ground. She blinked furiously to steady her blurring vision and saw the beast charging towards her.

Her sword was gone, her head was still spinning, and she was frozen to the ground. There was no time or way to protect herself. The Crystal Beast roared as it raised its fists above its head and Christina prepared herself for the blow that would end it all. But before its fists could crush her, there was an explosion of white light and a wave of white fire washed over the area. The beast in front of Christina roared and staggered to its knees, burning from head to toe. She looked around and saw the other beasts burning and dropping as well. Within moments, they shrank to the size of children, the fires died down, and the boys underneath the ice ran away, scared and confused.

Christina rubbed her temple then shook her head as her vision blurred back to focus. She pressed her hands against the ice on her legs and released wave after wave of white fire onto them. It took an entire minute to melt enough of the ice to free herself, but when she did, she jumped to her feet, ran to her sword, then rushed to Nana, lying a short distance away.

"Nana!" she cried, kneeling at her side. "Are you alright? Tell me you're okay. Tell me you're okay."

Nana forced a smile, but from the sadness in her eyes and how limp her arms and her legs were, it was evident that she was not okay. Fuji lay at her side and whimpered as he nestled his head under her hand.

"This..." she breathed. "...is where your journey begins...child."

"No," Christina said. "You can't do this!"

"Melt the mountain," Nana whispered. "Kill the serpent."

"I need you! You can't die!" Christina gripped Nana's body in her arms and pulled her closer to her chest.

Nana took a slow, deep breath before her next words. "Fire never really dies...it only...changes..." Then, with Christina still clutching her, Nana's body transformed before her very eyes. Her skin turned from brown to gray then to black. Cracks formed across her face and as a breeze whistled past, her body burst into a pile of ashes and was blown away with the wind, leaving nothing but her cloak in Christina's hands.

Christina hugged the now empty cloak and buried her face into it, washing it with her tears.

You can only imagine how devastating this was for her. It's a terrible thing for a child to lose their parents like Christina had. It was equally terrible to lose the person who had replaced her parents. She wondered if she could have prevented this by fighting harder. Maybe if she had listened to Nana in the first place and been ready to fight, she could have been able to beat the beasts. Maybe if she had used her sword earlier. Or maybe if she had finally mastered blue fire this time she could have used it on the beasts. Her mind swelled with all the mistakes she had made and the things she could have done better that would have kept Nana alive.

She wept deep into the night and it seemed that even the moon itself wept with her. Fuji howled in grief beside her until her sobs and his howling blended into a chorus of sadness.

Eventually the Sun began to rise and as it did, Nana's words rose in Christina's memory: *This is where your journey begins.*

Christina sniffled. Nana wouldn't want her to stay and blame herself. She would want her to move forward. There was so much Christina still needed to learn, so much she needed to see, but there was no time now. For now there was so much she needed to do.

With that, Christina stood to her feet, slid her sword into its scabbard, then pulled her hood tightly over her head. Fuji sniffed Nana's cloak on the ground, whimpered one last time, then stood at Christina's side, ready to follow her. Christina took a deep breath, faced the sunrise, then marched out of the tundra. For now, as Nana had said, her journey had begun.

Epilogue

Meanwhile, several villages away, Jonathan was practicing his own fighting on the edge of an ice cold stream. He lifted his hands and two pillars of water rose from the stream in front of him. With a flick of his wrists, the pillars snapped to the left like liquid whips. He spun his hands in circles and the water pillars whirled into two floating spirals then froze into two giant balls of ice. He slapped his hands together and the ice shattered into a cloud of snowflakes.

"Impressive," Joanna said as she came up behind him.

He paused and turned to see her holding a wooden bowl of soup.

"I made you something," she told him. "Let me know what you think. I'm experimenting with some new spices I found today."

"My sister is experimenting again," Jonathan chuckled, eyeing the soup in the bowl. It was brown with several black and green leaves floating around inside it with some chunks of meat bobbing up and down as well. "It's not gonna kill me, is it?"

Joanna scoffed. "Just tell me what you think."

Jonathan grabbed the bowl from her hands and shrugged. "Here goes nothing." Then he lifted it to his lips.

"Wait!" Joanna shouted. "It might be really spicy. You should have some cold water ready just in case."

Jonathan raised an eyebrow at her. "Cold water? You know I don't drink that. I'm not a Crystal Lord." Then he lifted the bowl to his lips again and took a sip. The instant he did, his eyes bulged open wide, he shoved the bowl back into his sister's hands, rushed to the stream, and thrust his face into the water.

Joanna watched in shock as he chugged water from the stream desperately. After what felt like several minutes, he finally stood and turned to her, his chest heaving.

"I'm sorry," Joanna said, but she couldn't stop herself from laughing. "I told you to be careful. Was it really that--" She stopped when she noticed that her brother wasn't laughing. As a matter of fact, his nostrils were flaring, he was hunched over like a cat about to pounce, and he was snarling at her.

"Are you okay?" she asked.

"Why would you do that?!" he shouted. "Are you trying to kill me?!"

"No!" Joanna cried, holding her hands up. "Why would you think that?"

She saw a glimmer of green light flash across his eyes and he rushed towards her, reaching to grab her throat. But she was quicker and slipped around him before he could touch her.

"Snap out of it, Jonathan!" she shouted. He turned and rushed towards her again and she threw a fireball at his chest. He grunted from the burn and stopped before reaching her.

She stood there confused and watched as he shook his head and wiped his eyes.

"What...what just happened?" he asked, looking around.

"You tried to attack me," Joanna explained, still eyeing him carefully.

He looked at her then at the stream then at the bowl that Joanna had dropped in the snow when he'd lunged at her.

They both looked at each other at the same time as the same thought occurred to them.

"The water," they said in unison.

"It made you aggressive," Joanna went on. "But why today? You drink water every day."

"Not cold water, remember?" Jonathan corrected. "It must only be cold water." His eyes widened as everything came together in his ming. "That's it! It's cold water! Cold water is what's controlling boys and making them so aggressive."

"But how?" Joanna asked.

Jonathan put his fingers to his lips and flicked his tongue curiously. He had drank quite a bit of water and had been surprised at himself. But what had surprised him even more was that he had tasted something else in the process.

"There's something in the water," he said.

"What?" Joanna asked him.

He glanced down at the snake bite on her hand before replying with one word: "Venom."

Made in the USA
Lexington, KY
16 November 2019